MERRY EX-MAS

A SMALL-TOWN SECOND CHANCE HOLIDAY ROMANCE

KAYE KENNEDY

DEDICATION

To all those authors who've struggled with burnout.

It isn't easy to keep the creativity well full, but you made it another year, and there are still plenty of stories within you that need to be told.

Keep going. You've got this. Be proud of yourself, because I'm proud of you!

NOTE FROM THE AUTHOR

Merry Ex-Mas!

I can't thank you enough for choosing to read Laurel and Jake's love story. If this is the first of my books you've picked up, welcome! I typically write dramatic full-length novels featuring everyday heroes in uniform set in a big city, so this lighthearted, small-town romance is a bit different, but hopefully it makes you want to check out my first responder world, too.

This eleventh hour holiday story came about when I had a bit of a freak out because I hadn't reached my publishing goal for the year. Refusing to end 2023 having only released one book, I pulled out my laptop and birthed this story.

This was a rough year. Early on I had to contend with some challenging medical diagnoses, and that, amongst other challenges, really derailed me. The prevalence of burnout in a creative industry such as writing is staggering.

Most authors are readers, too, so we struggle big time when we can't deliver the books we planned. The last thing we want to do is disappoint our readers. Living in that mindset, doesn't make getting the words down any easier, though. We can't write because we're stressed, and we're stressed because we can't write. It's a vicious cycle.

That's how this book came to be. I needed to break the cycle, and the best way I know how to do that is to write a story that I *want* to write, not one that I feel stressed about having to write. And I couldn't think of a better way to do that than with this quirky Hallmark-esque story. Now, I have this exciting new world of Evergreen Falls to play in!

The dopamine hit of this accomplishment has helped me shake off my writers' block, and now I can say that I've published two books this year, which, for whatever reason, makes me feel better about myself.

If you're reading this around the holidays, I wish you and your family a joyous season filled with love and laughter. If you're reading this during a different time of the year, I hope the message of finding balance in life and setting your priorities straight resonates, because it certainly doesn't have to be Christmas for us to be reminded of what's truly important.

I hope you enjoy reading this as much as I enjoyed writing it!

HUGS & HAPPILY EVER AFTERS,

Kaye Kennedy

ONE

My office was feeling less like a sanctuary and more like a prison cell with each passing day. I let out a breath as I took in the gray winter clouds outside my window, which blocked my view of the Manhattan skyscrapers beyond the glass. The dreary weather echoed the overall tone of my overwhelm.

"Laurel," my boss, Alan, barked as he stormed past my office. "I need those depositions before you leave tonight. No excuses."

I clenched my jaw and forced myself to reply, "Yes, sir." I was the newest senior associate at our firm—and, at twenty-eight, I was also the youngest—yet Alan treated me like I was one of his paralegals. And because he was a partner, there wasn't a darn thing I could do about it.

As he continued passed, I jotted the task down on my overflowing to-do list. I'd already stayed late every night for the past month preparing for my big trial right after Christmas. My eyes burned from staring at legal documents until the wee hours, and my back ached from hunching over my desk. While I had a team of associates and paralegals at my disposal to assist me, this was the first case I'd been assigned to lead since my promotion, so I was more hands-on with it than I was required to be.

I took a moment to rub my burning eyes. I was desperately in need of a break—a chance to breathe and remember there was more to life than billable hours and angry clients. *I'll get a break next week after the trial.* I blew out a breath and glanced at the picture of my parents on my desk. Mom's warm eyes and Dad's jovial grin, arm-in-arm behind the counter of our family's three-generation diner, seemed to beckon me home. This time of year always made me miss Evergreen Falls. The holidays in my small upstate New York hometown were magical. Twinkling lights lined Centre Street, leading to the Village Square where a centuries old evergreen stood tall, dressed in colored lights and glittering ornaments. I hadn't been home for Christmas since I was an undergrad, but if I closed my eyes, I could still smell the crisp, clean air laced with hot cocoa and pine.

The intercom on my phone buzzed. "Laurel, depos. Yesterday," Alan's nasally voice yanked me away from my memories.

"Working on it." I opened the file on my computer and dropped the depositions into our secure drive. After emailing it to my boss, I picked up my red pen and crossed that task off my list. Normally, that would bring me some sense of accomplishment, but I felt no relief.

I eyed the other picture frame beside my monitor, which held my younger sister's latest Christmas card. She smiled proudly, with her hand on my niece's shoulder, while her husband held my two-year-old nephew. The kids had gotten so big since I'd last seen them over Memorial Day. Guilt panged in my gut as I forced myself to refocus on my to-do list. A lot of it was busy work that I technically could delegate to my team, but that would require I loosen the reins a bit. *If I do, I could probably make it home for Christmas.*

Who was I kidding? I quickly dismissed that thought. My trial was three days after Christmas, which seemed like a cruel joke on the part of the clerk's office, so even though our firm was closed for the next two days, making it a long weekend, driving four hours up north to see my family would be irresponsible.

Still...

I tapped my pen against the edge of my keyboard.

"Screw it." I tossed the pen and got to work breaking my tasks up for my team. This year, I was going home for the holidays. No more excuses.

By the time I got everything delegated and organized, my office was dark and empty. I tucked everything I thought I might need (and then some) into my backpack, then donned my coat and headed for the elevators. If I rushed, I could get home, pack, and be on the road by eight o'clock.

Outside, the streets were alive with the hustle and bustle of my fellow workaholics intermingled with the flock of seasonal tourists. The visitors were easy to spot; they crammed the sidewalks, pausing to take photos of every little thing, interrupting the flow of pedestrian traffic. The city lights reflected off the slick concrete as I trudged past store windows that were adorned with colorful holiday displays. When I'd first moved to Manhattan, I'd loved the festive spirit that emanated through every facet of the city. This year, however, the bright lights and joyous displays did little to inspire any holiday cheer in me.

My boots crunched the salt sprinkling the sidewalk as I navigated through the crowd of last-minute shoppers, who were wrapped up in their own worlds, clutching armfuls of department store bags. As I turned the corner onto my block, a cold wind whooshed at me, making my cheeks tingle, and I caught a whiff of hot pretzels and roasting nuts mixed with the exhaust fumes of the passing cars. It created a distinctly urban scent I'd long ago gotten used to.

"Ms. Mercer." The doorman at my building dipped his head as I approached.

"Hi, Frank." I paused for a moment to chat. "Are you ever going to call me, Laurel?"

"Pardon me, Ms. Mercer. Laurel." He and I'd been having this exchange ever since I'd moved in ten months ago.

"Do you have any holiday plans?"

He nodded. "My granddaughter is hosting Christmas this year at her house on Long Island."

"That sounds nice."

"How about you, Ms. Laurel?"

Close enough. I didn't bother to correct him. "Actually, I'm driving upstate tonight. Going to my hometown to surprise my family."

He reached for the handle on the door. "You'd better get on the road. I hear the weather may get bad later."

"Oh?" I'd been so fixated on making sure that I had everything in order for work, that I'd neglected to check the forecast. This time of year, that information was crucial for any kind of travel plans. "Thank you, Frank. Merry Christmas."

"You, too."

I hurried to the elevator and rode it up to the seventeenth floor. Once in my apartment, I tossed some clothes and toiletries into a duffel, not bothering to fold or organize anything neatly, nor change out of my work clothes for that matter. Then, I lugged my bags down to the garage and loaded them into the trunk of my Lexus. As I climbed inside and turned the ignition, an anxious excitement fluttered in my stomach.

As I pulled out of the garage, I shook away the nerves that plagued me whenever I returned to Evergreen Falls. I swallowed my fear of running into Jake, my disloyal first love—only love—and tried to focus on my eagerness to see my family. As I merged onto the parkway, leaving behind the towering skyscrapers, I pressed play on my audiobook, *How to Win Friends and Influence People*. It was an old favorite.

Before long, the bright lights of the city faded into the distance and were replaced by a vast darkness with only my headlights to shine the way. The farther I got from Manhattan, the lighter I began to feel. For the first time in a long while, the pressures of work dulled, and I could breathe deeply. "This is exactly what I need," I whispered into the dark.

As I approached the foothills of the Adirondack Mountains, dainty snowflakes swirled lazily outside my windshield. The promise of a white Christmas in Evergreen Falls kept me going, despite my car's horrible track record in wintry weather. I'd gone too far to turn back. The snow was a mesmerizing curtain of white, cocooning me in solitude. The outside world was muffled, leaving me with my wandering thoughts, and the promise of home. I'd missed the simplicity and quiet beauty of a snowy night. No blaring horns or crowds of strangers.

My mind drifted to holidays past and our town's long-standing tradition of caroling around the tree in the Village Square on Christmas night. After my sister, Aspen, and I opened presents, Dad would load us onto his ATV and drive us out to the sledding hill beside our elementary school. We'd meet up with all of our friends and talk about the cool things Santa had brought us. When I was old enough, Dad would let me drive the ATV while he and Mom stayed home with Grampy.

I blew out a breath at the thought of our family's patriarch. Last we spoke, Mom said his osteoarthritis had worsened to the point where he needed a wheelchair. He'd fallen a couple of times, so she and Dad were considering moving him to the firemen's home in the Hudson Valley—a benefit of his sixty-two years as an Evergreen Falls volunteer firefighter. While I'd heard it was nice, I was still uneasy with the idea.

My foot eased off the gas as I approached the exit, meaning I had about an hour to go until I arrived in Evergreen Falls. Steadily, the snowfall increased, reducing visibility on an already dark and winding backroad. I lowered the volume on my stereo and leaned forward, gripping the steering wheel tightly as I squinted into the stormy night. The windshield wipers worked furiously as I followed the twists and turns deeper into the mountains.

I let my speedometer drift down to twenty miles per hour, and murmured, "At this rate, I might be home in time for Christmas morning...in thirty-six hours."

As I settled into a comfortable pace, my mind wandered to my upcoming trial. I was defending a man my age who'd been involved in a bar fight and charged with assault. He had no priors and witnesses were conflicted as to who had started the altercation: my client or his alleged victim. My job was to prove it'd been self-defense.

I cleared my throat and launched into my opening argument. "My client, Mr. Stephen Kramer, is a twenty-eight-year-old architect who is married to his high school sweetheart, and they're expecting their first child in March.

Under my breath, I added, "Pause and look over at Mrs. Kramer sitting behind her husband, so that the jury will do the same." Then I continued, "On April twenty-seventh, Steve and his wife were out at Finnegan's Pub with some friends. You will hear testimony that while Steve was using the restroom, Mr. Bardish [gesture to where he's seated] a man not known to either my client, nor his wife, approached Mrs. Kramer and allegedly made inappropriate comments. Steve will testify that when he returned from the facilities, he saw Mr. Bardish speaking with his wife and noticed that she seemed uncomfortable. What followed was an altercation resulting in us being here today."

I tapped my finger against the steering wheel as I recalled the next part. "As we navigate through the details of this case, it is imperative to remember that the law allows individuals the right to defend themselves when faced with imminent danger. The incident in question occurred in the midst of a chaotic and tense situation at the bar, where emotions ran high, and the atmosphere was charged. The prosecution is going to argue that my client started the altercation resulting in Mr. Bardish's injuries.

"My client asserts that he acted in self-defense, a fundamental right that we all cherish and that the law upholds. In the heat of the moment, when confronted with a perceived threat, Steve's actions were a direct response to protect himself, and were not only justified, but necessary for his own safety. We will present evidence and witnesses that— oh, my God," I gasped as my hands jerked the wheel hard to the right.

The deer that had just bolted into the road stood frozen in place as my tires lost traction, sending my car into a fishtail. My heart galloped in my chest as I fought to regain control of my vehicle.

"No, no, no," I cried out as I cranked the wheel left and right to correct the skid. The guardrail separating the road from a steep drop down the mountain loomed in my periphery as I pumped the brakes. My body jostled as the car skidded off the road and dipped into the drainage ditch. Snow sprayed up over the hood and windshield, blotting the world out in white.

With my hands still clenched, bloodless, on the steering wheel, my breath came in panicked gulps. The rush of adrenaline had me trembling as I willed my heartbeat to slow so I could take stock of the situation.

"I'm alive," I whispered. "Holy moly."

After a few centering breaths, I released the wheel and opened my door. Well, I *tried* to open my door, but the snow only allowed it crack open a few inches. "Oh, come on," I groaned, as I failed to slide through the narrow opening. Sometimes I forgot that I wasn't skinny anymore. Thanks to too many late nights in the office, I ate *a lot* of takeout, which hadn't been kind to my waistline. But I wasn't going to allow my love for eggrolls stop me from getting out of my surely disabled vehicle, so I managed to wiggle over the center console and plopped into the passenger seat. "Please open," I murmured as I reached for the handle. This time, the door opened wide. I stepped out and my leg sunk up to my knee in the snow bank.

"Fantastic," I grumbled, wishing I'd changed out of my skirt because my tights had already soaked through. After some wiggling, I retracted my leg into the car and shut the door, savoring the heat. Outside, the snow continued to fall in billowing waves. Unsure as to whether or not my exhaust pipe was blocked, I reached over and pressed the button to kill the engine. While it would be nice to keep the heat pumping out, it wasn't worth the risk of filling the car with carbon monoxide.

Although I knew it'd be useless, I fished my cellphone off the floorboard where it'd landed in the crash. A small part of me held out hope that I'd have service, but one look at the *No Service* symbol confirmed I was truly on my own to figure this situation out. It was after eleven p.m., the night before Christmas Eve, and I was in a ditch on the side of a rural country road. The odds of anyone coming to my rescue were slim.

The isolation sunk in, sending a chill down my spine that had nothing to do with the dropping temperature or my wet leg. "Okay, Laurel. Figure this out." I took a moment to steady my nerves and assess the situation. The snow was really coming down. Heavy flakes swirled in the headlights' glow, muffling the dark forest around me. I would have to turn them off soon so my battery didn't completely die, but I was reluctant to be completely without light. There was no way I'd be driving out of that snowbank, and if my memory served me correctly, I was at least ten miles from the nearest town, so walking was out of the question.

My only hope was to wait for another car to come along —*if one comes along*—preferably before I froze to death. I hugged myself against the cold as the realization that I was stranded settled in. The isolation was palpable, almost smothering, as I peered down the empty stretch of road.

Get it together. I straightened my shoulders and lifted my chin. I'd sat beside dangerous criminals in courtrooms, surely I could handle a little snow. I reached into my backseat and grabbed the blanket that I kept there; it was a condition my grandpa had set for me when I'd gotten my license. I could practically hear his voice, "*Never drive in the mountains without a blanket to keep warm, matches to start a fire, or a..."* I gasped.

I perked up and contorted my body further so I could squeeze between my front seats, and reached into the back once more. "Come on. Where are you?" I felt around blindly until my hand connected with cool metal. "Thank you, Grampy."

I slid the switch on the flashlight, and it glowed to life, so I settled into my seat and turned off my headlights. My finger traced over the flashlight's switch. I'd have to conserve its battery, too. When a car came, I would need the light to signal the driver, so before I could overthink it, I slid the switch. The sudden darkness was jarring. Living in the city that never sleeps, I was never truly in the dark anymore. I adjusted the blanket to cover my legs and forced myself to focus on the road as I waited to be rescued.

I waited.

And waited.

After I'd rehearsed my opening argument five times, I was about to give up hope, when I heard the distant rumble of an engine. Flashlight in hand, I perked up and opened the door. My legs sank into the snow, but I hardly felt the cold as I scrambled to the edge of the road. Two bright headlights cut through the night air and I toggled my flashlight on and off to signal the driver for help.

The pickup truck pulled over, its tires crunching the snow, and I breathed out in relief. When the driver's door opened, my heart rate quickened. My career, coupled with my years in Manhattan, had made me overly cautious of strangers. It was after midnight and I was a damsel in distress, which made me the perfect prey. *Shoot.* I mentally chastised myself for not having grabbed my pocketknife—a gift from Grampy—out of my center console.

Heavy boots hit the road as a tall figure emerged from the truck. The man wore a thick winter coat with the hood pulled up, obscuring his face. The relief in my gut warred with my cautious mind.

"Are you alright?" he called out as he traversed the deep snow.

"There was a deer," I croaked. "I'm stuck."

"I see that," he replied as he closed the gap between us and pushed back his hood.

His voice...

No way.

He stepped forward and his headlights illuminated his face. The scruffy beard was new, but I'd recognize those comforting brown eyes anywhere. My lungs about seized from my sharp intake of cold air.

Jake.

TWO

This can't be happening. I closed my eyes and opened them again, hoping I was wrong. I wasn't. He was nearly to me when he paused and cocked his head. "Laurel?"

Like an idiot, I gave him an abrupt wave, and tried to sound casual, as though the guy who'd shattered my heart appearing out of the blue to rescue me wasn't a huge, massive deal. "Oh. Hi, Jake."

"Wow. What, uh, what are you doing here?" His voice still had that warm, gravelly tone that once made my knees weak.

Under the delusion that it would somehow disguise my weight gain, I straightened out my skirt. "Well, I was driving to Evergreen Falls, and..." I pointed toward the slope. "A deer..."

"Right." He shook his head and stepped closer, his eyes scanning me with surprise.

I pulled my jacket tightly closed. My heart drummed erratically against the confines of my ribs as I caught a whiff of him—sawdust with a hint of metallic sweat, the kind specific to when you wear a winter coat in the car with the heat on.

His gaze came to a halt on my barely-sheathed legs. "Are those tights? You planning to freeze out here?"

My cold cheeks grew warm. "I left straight from work. I didn't anticipate camping out in a snowbank during a blizzard."

His lips quirked up, hinting at a familiar crooked smile. "Still. Evergreen Falls in December? Have you been a city girl so long you've forgotten how cold it gets up here?"

My jaw tightened as I contemplated returning to my car and waiting for another rescuer, but I doubted I'd get so lucky as to encounter a second person crazy enough to be out in this weather. "As much as I value your fashion advice," I quipped, "it isn't helping me get my car out of the ditch."

He placed his gloved hands on his hips as he looked around me to assess the situation with my Lexus. "Yeah, sorry, but we're not getting that out of here tonight. Even with my snow tires, I've got shit traction in this, and you'll never get a tow truck to come all the way out here in these conditions."

"Great," I muttered under my breath.

"What were you even thinking trying to drive that thing in this storm? I'm shocked you made it this far."

I huffed. "I was thinking I wanted to surprise my family for Christmas if that's alright with you."

He held up his hands and his tone softened. "Look, I've had a long night and the conditions are really shitty, so I was gonna stop in Whippleton to wait out the storm. Come with me, and we can try to get your car out tomorrow."

I shifted my weight from foot-to-foot. The idea of

spending another second with Jake had me squeamish, but the snowfall was getting heavier, so I had no other choice.

Unless I want to risk freezing to death in this ditch.

I contemplated that for a moment, but before I could calculate how long it would take for my car to drop to a fatal temperature, Jake stepped around me, sinking his tan Carhartt coveralls into the bank. "I'll grab your bag. Is it in the trunk?"

"I can get it." I stumbled into the snow, which now passed my knees, and tried to get around him, but it was fruitless. The earth seemed determined to drag me into its depths.

"Get outta here, Laurel. You're gonna freeze."

Was he always this bossy?

"You used to like it."

"Excuse me?"

"My bossiness. Now, go sit in my truck and get warm."

My eyes widened; I hadn't realized I'd spoken out loud. Out of defiance, I cleared my throat and crossed my arms. As tempting as the allure of a warm vehicle was, I wasn't moving.

Jake suppressed a laugh as he felt around the rear of my car. "How the hell do you open this thing?"

I fished the key fob out of my pocket and pressed the release button. When it popped open, he reached in and hefted my Dior duffle over his shoulder. "This, too?" He held up my backpack and remarked, "Damn. You traveling with cinder blocks?"

"Careful with that, please. I have a trial next week. There's a lot of material to review."

"Haven't you lawyers ever heard of going paperless?"

So, he knows I'm a lawyer. Has he been keeping track of

me? I didn't have social media—that was hazardous with my job. As defense attorneys, for each person we helped, there were at least five more who hated us.

He shut my trunk. "Get in the truck, Laurel."

I stretched over to open the passenger side door, tossed my flashlight in, then clicked the lock button on my key fob. I clumsily twisted around and proceeded to stomp my way to his pickup. The familiar scent of earthy wood wafting from his cab reminded me of his father's hardware store. I would visit Jake there after school and on the weekends sometimes if I wasn't working at my family's diner. His dad would always scold him to stop being distracted and get back to work. I shook that thought from my mind. Seeing Jake was resurrecting memories better left buried under the snowdrifts.

I reached up and clutched the handle so I could launch myself into the truck—in the most graceful way one could *launch* one's self, of course. The warm air blowing out of the dash greeted me like a much-needed hug as I settled onto the cloth bench seat.

The driver's side door opened and Jake slid my bags over to me before he reached behind his seat and retrieved a water bottle, then tossed it my way. My reflexes served me better than I anticipated and I caught it. "Thanks," I said as a shiver worked its way through my thawing muscles.

"Welcome." He climbed up and got behind the wheel. "You hungry?"

"I'm fine." Truth? I hadn't eaten since breakfast, so I was starving, but I wasn't about to tell him that.

"You sure?"

"Positive." A nagging sense made me wonder if he was asking me because I was overweight. "Why?"

He glimpsed over his left shoulder at the roadway, then eased the truck forward. "I didn't see any tire tracks when I was driving, so I'm guessing you've been stuck here a while. I'd be hungry."

Oh. I unscrewed the water bottle and took a sip. "Well, I'm not."

"Okay."

The awkward silence that filled the cab made my skin prickle. "What are you doing out in this storm anyway?" I asked in an effort to break some of the tension.

Jake glanced at me briefly before returning his gaze to the road. "I'm a volunteer fireman in Evergreen Falls. We got a call from the Irvine department that they needed a few things to prep for the cleanup from this blizzard. They've been having funding issues. Anyway, I'm the newest lieutenant so I went."

I hummed. "Seems kind of risky to drive to Irvine in this weather."

"Not as risky as driving to Evergreen Falls from Manhattan in it."

Touché. I hadn't heard that Jake had joined the fire department, but it didn't surprise me. He'd always been the heroic, salt-of-the-earth type. The kind of guy who stopped to help a stranger change a flat tire; who never missed a day of work; who volunteered to drive an hour in a blizzard to help people he didn't know. Dependable. Steady.

Christmas classics played softly through the speakers, and Jake kept his eyes fixed on the road, his brow furrowed in concentration, as he navigated us through the mountain. His brights reflected off the blanket of snow that fell before us, reducing visibility to an alarmingly low level. As uncomfortable as it was to be stuck in a car with him, I was grateful to not be driving. Even if my Lexus hadn't wound up in a ditch, I likely would've had to pull over to wait the storm out.

I slid my hands under my thighs to warm them.

"You still chilly?"

"I'm defrosting."

He chuckled as he reached for the knob to turn up the heat. "You always did have cold hands and feet."

His chaffing sparked a pang of nostalgia in me. On many occasions, he used to tease me about my icicle limbs. I would roll my eyes and let him wrap me in his football jacket, breathing in his scent.

Now I just shifted awkwardly, the gulf between the old me and the new me feeling wider than ever. We lapsed into silence, the weight of our tangled history hanging in the air, as the truck crawled towards our destination. It took twenty minutes to get to Whippleton. It was nearly one in the morning, and the streets were deserted. A fresh blanket of snow glowed under the street lamps as Jake drove slowly down the main street, squinting to read the signs through the blizzard.

"I think that's the bed and breakfast," he said, nodding towards a quaint Victorian house with a sign that read *Creek View Inn*. He pulled into the driveway and turned to me. "Wait here. I'll see if they have any rooms." Jake crunched through the snow up to the front porch and rang the doorbell repeatedly until a light switched on inside. An elderly woman opened the door in her nightgown and curlers. They spoke briefly, and he gestured back to the truck. The woman eyed me curiously before nodding and disappearing inside, then emerging once more.

Jake turned and headed my way, swinging a key ring around his finger. "We're in luck." He reached over and turned the key in the ignition, killing the engine, then added, "One room left."

My lips parted to protest, but I thought better of it and snapped them shut. The odds of there being another place to stay in that sleepy town were slim, and the unrelenting snow made traveling much farther too risky. Jake grabbed my bags, then followed the craters his footsteps had made back up the walkway.

My stomach fluttered as I stepped out into the biting cold. We hurried inside the cozy inn, and were welcomed by the scent of gingerbread and cinnamon. After stomping the snow off our shoes, we removed them, then the older woman, who introduced herself as Lillian Foster, led us upstairs.

"Here you are, dears." She gestured toward a wooden white door with a gold number three hanging in the middle of a small red and gold ribbon wreath. "Breakfast is at eight, but it's late, so you two sleep in and I'll save you some. Sleep well," she said before shuffling back down the stairs in her pink slippers.

Jake inserted the old key and opened the door, then reached in and flicked on the light switch, revealing one double bed. My cheeks flushed as we stood awkwardly, the charged air crackling between us. He made the first move and entered while I lingered in the hall and watched as he placed my bags on the Americana-style quilt that was draped over the foot of the bed.

"You planning to sleep in the hallway?" he asked as he shrugged off his coat and hung it in the small closet.

With tentative steps, I entered the quaint space, closing the door behind me. The warm, navy carpet comforted my cold, wet feet. I busied myself examining the room, hyper-aware of Jake's presence behind me. A bowl of potpourri sat on the nightstand, giving the room a muted floral scent intermingled with a hint of smoke from the wood-burning stove I'd spotted in the living room downstairs. Landscape paintings of small-town America adorned the white shiplap walls, and a wooden flag hung above the bed, below which sat a row of plump, white pillows that looked particularly inviting after that harrowing drive.

"You can have the bed. I'll take the loveseat," Jake offered, nodding toward the small blue and white checkered sofa crammed in the corner.

"Oh, um, you don't have to..." I trailed off, unsure of how to navigate the situation.

"I don't mind," he replied as he unbuckled the straps on his coveralls.

I spun around to give him privacy and busied myself with hanging my jacket in the closet. Next to *Jake's*. The thought of that did strange things to my head. It didn't help that he was in an unknown state of undress behind me. I took my time smoothing the wrinkles out of my wool peacoat.

"You don't have to hide in the closet. I'm wearing clothes, I just wanted to get off the wet top layer."

"I wasn't hiding, I—" I spun around and lost my train of thought because Jake was standing there in jeans and a white t-shirt that made him look utterly delicious, and, frankly, that pissed me off. He'd always been an attractive boy, but as a man he was a stop traffic kind of handsome. Meanwhile, I didn't think I could even squeeze a calf into the pants I'd worn in high school. It wasn't fair how most men got hotter with age.

He flashed me a crooked grin. "You alright?"

"Great." I tugged on the bottom of my blazer.

"That color suits you."

I glanced down at the candy apple red jacket that made up half of my power suit. At five-foot-two, I had to use whatever tools I could to bolster my authority, particularly since I worked in an industry dominated by men. Plus, red was festive. "Oh. Umm, thank you."

"You're welcome." He took a seat on the sofa that was far too small for him. "I'm sorry if I was a dick earlier. It's been a long night and it's kind of wild running into you like this."

I flicked my wrist. "It's fine. I appreciate you coming to my rescue." With my arms crossed over my chest, I reclined against the wall. "And, yes, it was certainly surprising seeing you get out of that truck."

"So, how, umm, is city life treating you?"

"It's great," I fibbed. "My job is great. I've got a great group of friends. It's...great." My ears warmed. Surely seven years of higher education had given me a better vocabulary than that. Now that I'd finished embarrassing myself, a plethora of synonyms for the elementary word *great*, flooded my brain:

Exceptional.

Fantastic.

Extraordinary.

Wonderful.

Remarkable.

"That's...good."

At least Jake's vocabulary was as stunted as mine seemed to be...

"How about you? How's Evergreen Falls?"

He scratched his beard. "Can't complain. My dad retired, so I've taken over the store. That and the fire department keep me busy."

"I'm sure."

The silence hung between us like an unwelcomed party guest.

"I'm going to get ready for bed." I gestured toward the attached bathroom.

He nodded. "Go ahead."

I crossed to my luggage and retrieved my toiletry bag, as well as a pair of yoga pants and an oversized sweatshirt, then slipped into the restroom. As I brushed my teeth, I caught my reflection in the mirror. The expensive makeup I'd let the tart at the department store talk me into had held up well despite my ordeal. For half a second, I debated washing it off, but decided against that. Had I been home—alone—I would've, but being stuck in a room with Jake, there was no way I'd let myself be that vulnerable.

"I know," his voice carried through the wall and I paused my brushing. "Do you really think I'd miss spending Christmas Eve with my daughter?"

Daughter? Jake has a child?

I side-stepped closer and rested my ear against the door.

"I'll head home first thing," he continued. "Once I help Laurel get her car out."

My brows shot up. *He told his wife about me?* I wasn't sure how to feel about that. He had gloves on all evening, so I hadn't had a chance to check if he wore a wedding ring.

"Yeah, I hear you, but I can't very well leave her stranded now, can I?"

I couldn't blame his wife for not being happy he was with me. *Did he tell her we are sharing a room?* I would never be comfortable with my husband staying overnight with his ex. If I had one, that is.

"That was rhetorical. You weren't suppose to answer. It's late, I just wanted to let you know I wouldn't be home tonight so that you didn't worry. Get some sleep. I'll see you tomorrow."

Toothpaste dribbled down my chin and I wiped it with the back of my hand.

"Love you, too."

That stung. I swallowed, forgetting about the mouthful of toothpaste, and sputtered a cough.

"You alright in there?" he called out.

I spit into the sink. "Fine," I replied with fake joy in my tone. He was the only man I'd ever loved, and while it was irrational to believe the same was true for him, that delusion had gotten me through the past decade. I cupped my hand, filled it with water from the faucet, then rinsed my mouth out while I contemplated my conflicting feelings about Jake. All of my good memories with him were tainted by his betrayal.

Once I was finished getting ready for bed, I took a steadying breath before re-entering the bedroom. Jake was reclined on the loveseat; his calves hung up and over the armrest.

"You can't sleep like that," I commented as I stuffed my dirty clothes into my bag. "You can take the bed."

"It's all good." He turned to look at me, and the heat of his gaze made me squirm. I tugged on the bottom of my sweatshirt to make sure it covered my hips.

"I'm smaller. It makes more sense for me to—"

"Do you always sleep in makeup?"

I recoiled, taken aback by his abrupt subject change. "Excuse me?"

He gestured to my face. "You left your makeup on."

My heart clamored in my chest as I searched my brain for a response. "Oh, I forgot. I'm tired." I lifted my bags off the bed and deposited them on the floor.

Jake flipped onto his side, bending his knees to fit the space. "I've always liked your freckles, you know."

I blinked. The freckles that peppered my nose and cheeks made me look juvenile, so I'd gotten into the habit of covering them with foundation. Ignoring him, I went around to the side of the bed, and peeled the sheets back.

"Sorry. I didn't mean to make you uncomfortable."

"You didn't," I lied. "But your wife probably wouldn't appreciate you complimenting me." I regretted the words the moment they left my lips, but the deflection worked.

He sat up. "My wife?"

I climbed into bed and covered myself with the blankets. "I accidentally overheard you on the phone. Your voice carries. I bet she isn't thrilled that you're here with me instead of being home with her and your daughter. I didn't know you had a kid." I fluffed the pillows behind me. "Unless you've made cheating a habit, in which case maybe she isn't surprised that you're here," I added with a bite in my tone.

"You've gotta be fucking kidding me. We're really gonna do this now?" He snickered as he ran a hand over his beard. "First of all, there's a lot you don't know about me because it's been a decade since you've seen or spoken to me. If you'd been around, you would know about my daughter and the fact that I'm a single dad because every attempt I've made to date since you has failed miserably. It was my *mom* I was talking to on the phone."

A twisted up piece of me was glad to hear he hadn't had any success with dating either, and that it wasn't just me.

"Second, I never cheated on you."

I shook my head with disdain. "All these years, and you still can't admit it?"

He threw his hands up. "There's nothing to admit!

Hailey set me up. She wanted me for herself, so she planned to have you walk by us at that party. Like I told you back then, *she* kissed *me*. Had you stuck around long enough, you would've seen me push her off."

"I'd seen enough," I replied as a laid down on my side with my back to him. "And with Hailey, of all people. You knew what a wench she was to me in high school."

"You wanna know what I think? I think you saw what you wanted to see. You were leaving for college a few days after that, and you didn't want to be saddled with a boyfriend back home."

"What?" Outraged, I flipped over and met his gaze as I sat up. "That's completely ridiculous."

"Is it? Or does it explain why you wouldn't listen to reason back then any more than you're willing to listen to it now?"

I huffed. "You cheat on me with my mortal enemy, yet I'm the bad guy here?"

"No one's the bad guy. Except for maybe Hailey, but she has since apologized for everything."

"Oh, so you're friends with her now?" Her name alone still sent a chill through me. Hailey Jennings had ruined my life. At least, it'd felt like that back then.

Sometimes, it still did.

He blew out a breath. "Laurel..."

My eyes widened. "So you are. Wow."

His gaze dropped to his knees. "Like I said, you've been gone a long time. There's a lot you don't know."

"Right. Well, for the record, I never wanted to end things between us, so you're wrong about that. I was actually planning on unenrolling in Penn State and registering at one of the state schools up here instead because the closer it got to me leaving, the worse I felt about having to leave you."

He glanced up, and my attention dropped to the cuticle I was picking at before I continued, "I was planning on telling you that the night of the party, but then I saw you with *her*, so yeah..."

In my periphery, I noticed him stand, then he walked over and sat on the edge of the bed. "You weren't going to leave?"

A shake of my head was about all I could manage in response because this conversation had brought the heartache back and I refused to let him see me cry.

"But Penn State was your dream school."

I shrugged.

"I never would've let you give that up for me."

"It wasn't your choice," I whispered as I scratched at my cuticle.

Jake let out a sigh. "I swear to you—on my daughter—I never cheated on you. I love you."

My chin shot up to look at him.

He cleared his throat. "Loved you. I *loved* you." There was genuine earnestness in his warm brown eyes. "Please believe me."

I took a deep breath in and let it out. This conversation was too much for me, so I decided to shut it down. "It's late. We should get some sleep."

"Laurel..."

I laid back down and turned over so I didn't have to see him, and said, "I've had a stressful day. Besides, that was a long time ago. It doesn't matter anymore. Please, Jake, let's just go to bed."

The sound of his breathing echoed in my ears, then I felt the mattress spring up and heard his footsteps as he went to shut off the light before returning to his spot on the sofa.

As I closed my eyes, Jake's ardent denial echoed in my mind, clashing with my own lingering doubts. All those years, I'd been angry with him for betraying me. That anger was the only thing that made missing him tolerable. Without it...well...

There was a reason Jake was the only man I'd ever loved...but that was a door best left closed.

THREE

The sunlight streaming through the window caused me to wake with a start on the unfamiliar hard bed. For the briefest of moments, I'd forgotten where I was, but as I took in my surroundings, my memory of the night before hit me like a giant sack of potatoes. I sat up and turned toward the source of the light. The world outside my window was a winter wonderland. Whippleton transformed into a picturesque snow globe overnight. I blinked at the sheer volume of snow. Judging by what I could see of the lamp posts, there had to be at least four feet blanketing the ground.

Snowbound on Christmas Eve, how perfectly inconvenient.

Glancing over at Jake, still sound asleep, I couldn't help but admire his peaceful expression, but I was still unsure what to make of our last conversation. Careful not to disturb him, I folded back the blanket, tiptoed out of the room, and made my way downstairs, motivated by my grumbling stomach. I hadn't eaten in twenty-four hours.

Creek View Inn was enchanting, with garlands and

twinkling fairy lights weaving through the banister, giving off the warmest glow. The scent of cinnamon and ginger-bread still filled the air, but this time it was intermingled with maple syrup, tempting me toward the kitchen. Mrs. Foster, the innkeeper, greeted me with a smile as she turned off the sink where she was washing dishes.

"Good morning. I hope you slept well."

"Yes, thank you," I replied as I followed my nose to the coffee pot.

"Help yourself, dear. I'll fix you a plate."

"Thank you." I filled a Christmas mug with coffee, then stirred in two sugars.

"Isn't it beautiful outside?" Mrs. Foster mused, gesturing to the snow-covered landscape beyond the window, before plugging in the waffle iron.

"Undeniably," I agreed, though the beauty did little to assuage my unease. "Do you think we'll be able to get out today?"

She shook her head. "I'm afraid that isn't likely. The roads haven't been cleaned yet, so you two might be stuck here for the day. We got nearly forty inches last night. That could be a new record."

"Great," I muttered under my breath, regretting the impulsivity of my decision to go home for the holiday.

"But don't worry. Your room is available tonight, and I'm planning a Christmas Eve feast for all of the guests."

"Morning, ladies," Jake's voice interrupted my thoughts as he entered the kitchen. He glanced at the snow outside, and cursed under his breath, concern etched on his face. "Guess we're not going anywhere, huh?"

"Seems that way," I replied, before savoring a sip of the hot coffee.

He turned toward Mrs. Foster. "Does it usually take long for the roads to get cleared here?"

The elderly woman poured batter onto the hot iron. "I expect they'll have this main strip done in the next few hours since the annual Whippleton Gingerbread House Competition is at the town hall this afternoon. As for the rest of the roads, those will likely be done tomorrow." She closed the waffle iron and flipped it over. "Although, with the holiday..."

Jakes face paled.

Mrs. Foster wiped her hands on her apron. "After I make you kids some breakfast, I can call my son. He works for the town, so he should be able to give us an estimate."

"Thank you," Jake replied as he poured himself coffee.

I pulled my phone out of the kangaroo pocket of my sweatshirt to find zero bars. Anxiety soured my stomach. "Do you have wi-fi here?" It was after nine, so I was sure my boss had already tried calling me a few times.

"We do." She flipped the iron back over, then fished the waffle out and put it on a plate before pouring more batter. "But I'm afraid the storm has knocked it out."

I grumbled as I eyed my utterly useless phone.

"We have a landline you can use," she said as she closed the iron and flipped it over once more.

Jake added, "I have service, too, if you want to call your family."

"It's just my boss—never mind. I'll let you know. Thanks." I slid my cell back into my pocket. If I called from an upstate area code, Alan would know I'd left the city. Being that we were only a few days out from the trial, he would freak if he discovered where I was.

"What do you need to call your boss for?" Jake asked as he stirred in the creamer. "It's Christmas."

"I told you I have a trial coming up."

He clinked the spoon against the rim of his mug, then set it on a dish. "So that means you have to work through the holiday?"

I scoffed. "There's no such thing as a holiday in my line of work."

Seeming to notice my distress, Jake pulled out the chair beside me, took a seat, and softened his tone. "I'm sure your boss will understand if you don't answer your phone because it's Christmas and you're snowed in."

"Easy for you to say. You don't know my boss." Cradling my mug, I inhaled.

"You can sit around here and sulk, or we can make the best of it. I'm missing Christmas Eve with my daughter, but I'm not gonna sit around here and stew all day." The mention of his daughter brought a flicker of sadness to his eyes.

I sipped my coffee. "Sorry." Suddenly my work stress didn't seem so bad. "Like you said, we'll make the best of it."

Mrs. Foster placed a plate in front of each of us, and with a knowing smile, said, "Ah, I have just the thing to brighten your spirits!"

"These waffles do smell fantastic," Jake replied as he picked up his fork.

"Thank you. The maple syrup is fresh from a local farm."

I savored the heavenly scent of creamy butter mixed with the sticky syrup, powdered sugar, and brightly-colored berries sitting before me. As eager as I was to dig in, a tinge of self-consciousness got the better of me. The thought of Jake watching me eat something so indulgent made me uneasy.

"But I wasn't talking about breakfast," Mrs. Foster

continued. "You two should enter the gingerbread house contest. It's a beloved holiday tradition around here."

"Us?" I asked skeptically as I plucked a strawberry off the top of the waffle. "Make a gingerbread house together?"

"Absolutely! It's a wonderful way to pass the time, and you might even win a prize," Mrs. Foster replied with enthusiasm.

I glanced at Jake who was chewing a bite of his waffle. He turned to the older woman and said, "Adalyn, my daughter, loves gingerbread." Then he looked at me. "It could be fun."

Fun was not the word I would have chosen to describe my feelings about building a gingerbread house with Jake, but it would serve as a much-needed distraction from my professional woes, so I found myself reluctantly agreeing. "I suppose we could give it a try."

"Excellent. You'll need to be at the town hall in an hour to register," Mrs. Foster explained before leaving us to our breakfast.

A tense quiet befell us, filled only with the clanking of Jake's silverware. One by one, I picked at the berries, unsure of what to say. We hadn't exactly ended our talk the night before on a high note.

"Do you have something against waffles?" Jake asked before stabbing a piece with his fork.

"Sugar and carbs aren't on my diet."

His eyes narrowed. "Why are you dieting? You look great."

I nearly spit out the coffee I'd just sipped. *He can't be serious.* "Nice try."

"What?" he asked around a mouthful of waffle. "You do. In high school, you were so skinny. A little meat looks good on your bones."

I blinked. *A little meat?*

"It's a compliment, Laurel. Now, eat the waffle. I can hear your stomach growling from here."

My cheeks flushed. Desperate for a subject change, I picked up my fork, and asked, "How old is your daughter?"

"She's six."

I did some quick math. When Jake had become a father, I'd been in my first year of law school. That was a crazy thought. "I'm really sorry you're missing Christmas Eve with her."

He shrugged. "I'll get to see Adalyn in the morning. She's playing the Virgin Mary in the Christmas pageant at her school." His face lit up with pride.

"That's adorable."

"So let's hope the roads get cleared soon, because I *can't* miss that. I'll start walking now if I have to."

"It'll get done. You're not walking all the way to Evergreen Falls. I'll drive over with you and help shovel along the way if need be."

He gave me a crooked grin. "Thanks."

"Of course." I cut a piece of the waffle and put it in my mouth. The decadence caused me to let out a tiny moan.

Jake chuckled. "Good, right?"

I finished chewing. "This might be the best waffle I've ever had."

"I don't know. The ones we used to make for the pancake breakfast in high school were pretty good."

I let out a laugh as I recalled the annual fundraiser the football team did. The pancake and waffle batter came out of a box, yet somehow the guys always seemed to make them taste like cardboard. "Yeah, right. Those were barely edible."

A mischievous gleam filled his eyes. "If that's so, then why'd you come every year?"

"It definitely wasn't because of the breakfast." I cut off another piece of waffle. Back then, I'd gone pretty much anywhere Jake went.

"Good to know." His knife squeaked against the plate.

"Like you didn't already know."

He shrugged a shoulder. "Maybe I just wanted to hear you say it."

Is he flirting? Couldn't be. I shook my head of that notion as I took another bite.

He finished his plate and put it in the sink. "I hate to bail, but if we're gonna go to this thing. I've gotta shower. I've had these same clothes on since yesterday morning."

I'd been too consumed by the absurdity of the previous night's situation that it hadn't dawned on me that Jake hadn't planned on spending the night away from home, so he didn't have anything with him. "It's fine," I replied. "You can use my toiletries if you need."

"Thanks. I think I've got a change of clothes in my truck, so I'm gonna grab those, then head up. I'll be quick so you can get in there."

"Okay."

His eyes held mine for a beat too long, then he echoed, "Okay." He turned and exited the kitchen, leaving me to ponder what the heck I was doing. The last thing I needed was to spend any time with Jake Hansen. I should be focusing on my case and doing something—anything—to get out of there.

Instead, I finished my waffle, then went upstairs to get ready for a gingerbread house competition.

. . .

"ADALYN WOULD LOVE THIS. Maybe I'll bring her next year," Jake said as he coated the roof of our house with icing.

The mental image of Jake building a gingerbread house with his little girl made my uterus clench, so I focused on picking the red and green gumdrops out of the bag to use as shingles. When I'd been promoted to senior associate, I'd accepted the fact that I would never be a mom. Taking time off from the practice would be career suicide. The way I figured, if I could endure Alan for a few more years, I'd have a real shot at making partner. My dedication to my job was what had gotten me to where I was so far, and I hadn't worked that hard just to have it all crumble.

"You good?" Jake asked before popping a red gumdrop into his mouth.

"Great. Why?" *Here I go with the vocabulary again.*

"You got quiet."

"Did I?" My voice squeaked.

Jake let out a muted laugh. "Yeah."

"Are you done icing the roof so I can put these on?"

He stepped aside. "Go for it."

I began alternating the colored gumdrops while Jake sprinkled shredded coconut on the front lawn to mimic snow. As we worked on constructing our gingerbread house, we fell into a comfortable rhythm. It was almost like a decade hadn't passed at all. The tension between us dissolved, and was replaced by laughter and good-natured rivalry.

Jake took a step back and hummed.

"What?" I asked as I placed York Peppermint Patties down to form a walkway.

"Your tree..."

"What about my tree?" I'd constructed a Christmas tree on the lawn using green Twizzlers.

"It's crooked."

"No, it isn't." I dropped the chocolates and stepped back to assess. I tilted my head from side to side. "It's perfectly symmetrical. I think your head is crooked."

Jake busted out in laughter. "I know. I just wanted to freak you out."

I huffed and swatted his arm playfully. "Seriously, Jake?"

"You're taking this so seriously."

I resumed placing the stones, making sure to space them out evenly. "You know I'm a perfectionist."

"Oh, I'm aware." He picked up the icing bag. "Don't forget to have fun, too." He squeezed the bag and white icing landed square on my chest.

"Jake," I squealed, drawing attention from the other contestants.

"Loosen up, Laur."

"Fine." I scooped the icing off my shirt and flung it at his face. "Bullseye," I exclaimed victoriously as I eyed the paste in his beard.

A playful sparkle lit up his eyes as he grabbed a fistful of cocoa powder, then blew it straight out of his hand and into my face.

"Oh, now it's on." I picked up some M&M's and pelted him with them.

He held up his hands. "Okay, okay. I concede."

"Does that mean I win?" I held up an M&M.

A smile filled his face. "You win."

I tossed the candy into my mouth. "Good."

Jake handed me a paper towel, and my hand brushed his, sending a zing up my arm.

"Thanks." I blotted the cocoa off my face.

"You're welcome." He retrieved another towel and tried to clean off his beard.

"Let me help." I took the paper from him and used it to wiped the sticky icing.

His eyes met mine and I paused. An old familiarity hit me in the heart, and if I wasn't mistaken, there was hope in his expression.

"Fifteen more minutes," the organizer announced, breaking our reverie.

I stepped back and cleared my throat. "I should put up the fence."

"I'll finish the chimney."

We worked diligently as the clock ran down.

"Jake," I murmured, as I carefully positioned candy canes around the house. "Thank you for today. I needed this." I couldn't remember the last time I'd done something just for fun.

"Me too," he replied softly, his eyes meeting mine. "We make a pretty good team, don't we?"

"We always have," I conceded, my heart swelling with warmth. For once, I allowed myself to ponder on what could have been had Jake and I never gone our separate ways.

FOUR

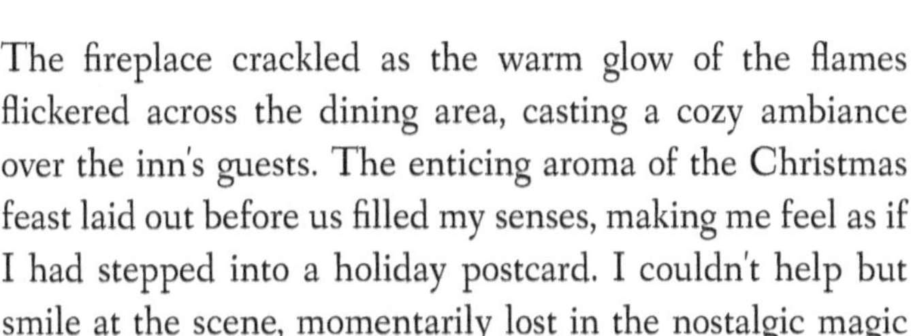

The fireplace crackled as the warm glow of the flames flickered across the dining area, casting a cozy ambiance over the inn's guests. The enticing aroma of the Christmas feast laid out before us filled my senses, making me feel as if I had stepped into a holiday postcard. I couldn't help but smile at the scene, momentarily lost in the nostalgic magic of a small-town Christmas.

"You two are so cute together," Leslie, a middle-aged woman who was also a guest at the Creek View Inn gushed from across the table. Her cheeks were rosy with the warmth of the room and the mulled wine she'd been sipping.

I began to protest, "Oh, we—"

"Thank you," Jake interjected as he patted my thigh beneath the table, sending shockwaves through my body.

He was right. These strangers didn't need to know our story. After we'd competed in the competition together—and came in third, much to our surprise—everyone had assumed we were together anyway. Sometimes, it was easier to simply let people believe whatever they wanted.

I cleared my throat as I reached for my wine. "Yes, thank you." I tried to sound genuinely appreciative while fighting the heat that crept into my cheeks. Beside me, Jake shifted his weight slightly, his elbow brushing against mine.

"Indeed," Leslie's husband, Rob, chimed in, raising his glass of eggnog in our direction. "To Jake and Laurel, may your love always be..." He puckered his lips in thought before finishing, "So carefree."

Jake lifted his drink first, and I followed.

"Cheers," the other guests echoed as we all clinked glasses, the sound reverberating through the room like the ringing of sleigh bells.

"That's very kind of you," Jake said, his eyes meeting mine for a brief, charged moment. The subtle tension between us was palpable, and the compliments, well-intentioned as they were, only served to exacerbate it. It was as if each kind word nudged us closer to confronting the undeniable chemistry that had been exponentially growing between us over the course of the day.

"You two remind me of my Johnny and me when we were your age," Hilda, a silver-haired, grandmotherly woman, remarked before turning to her husband. "Don't they?"

"Sure," he replied without looking up from the ham he was devouring.

Seemingly unfazed by her husband's lack of enthusiasm, she asked, "Tell us, how did you two meet?"

Jake patted his mouth with the hunter green cloth napkin. "We grew up together."

Leslie clutched a hand to her chest. "Oh, how adorable. True sweethearts. You don't see much of that these days."

"So very true," Hilda replied before urging, "Go on."

Jake glanced my way, but must've realized I had no

intention of responding, so he continued. "We didn't start dating until high school. I wanted to sooner, but—"

"My parents wouldn't let me date until I was fifteen," I finished for him, recalling what a fight that had been after Jake had asked me to the eighth-grade dance, and I'd had to say no.

"We set the same rule for our daughter." Rob speared a green bean with his fork. "We're meant to be at her house down in Westchester right now, but the storm." He gestured toward the window.

Mrs. Foster interjected, "My son says the roads should be clear by morning, so you'll all be able to get to your destinations."

That was a relief. While the past day hadn't turned out to be the complete disaster I'd anticipated, I was still eager to get to Evergreen Falls, particularly for Jake's sake.

Leslie swirled her mug of mulled wine. "Do you two have kids?"

"No," I replied with a shake of my head at the same time that Jake said, "Yes."

Leslie hummed. "Curious."

"Jake has a daughter." I reached for my wine. With each sip, the atmosphere seemed to grow warmer, more intimate.

A flock of confused eyes stared our way.

I added, "We broke up after high school when I left for college."

"We recently reconnected." Jake draped his arm behind my chair, and I stilled.

Hilda tapped her fingertips together and cooed. "I love a good second chance romance. That's what we call it in the book world. I was a librarian for forty-three years."

"That must've been an interesting profession," I commented in an effort to deflect their attention.

"It was. Continue," she urged.

Jeez, these people won't quit. I drained my wine. "As Jake said, we recently reconnected, and we're seeing where things go."

He nodded beside me. "Right."

The guests continued to stare; the women in particularly seemed to be on the edges of their seats.

"I'm a lawyer in Manhattan, and Jake still lives in our hometown, Evergreen Falls."

"Long distance is rough," Rob chimed in. "Meeting here in the middle for Christmas, are ya?"

"Something like that." I reached for the bottle of merlot and refilled my glass.

Leslie tsked. "Here you two are trying to have a romantic getaway and we're crashing it."

"It's fine." I pushed my mostly empty plate back. "Really." The more time we spent with them, the less time I had to be alone with Jake, which, while certainly less awkward than it'd been initially, was still a bit weird.

"Nonsense." Hilda reached over and shoved the cork into the wine bottle. "Take this up to your room and have a passionate evening."

Mrs. Foster stood. "I'll make you a plate of cookies to bring up with you."

"That won't be necessary." I glanced at Jake and gave him a look that should've urged him to help me out, but he didn't.

Instead, he smirked and said, "A quiet evening alone sounds nice. Doesn't it, sweets?"

His use of the old term of endearment he'd used for me when we'd dated transported me back to high school. Our eyes locked and my breathing slowed. Jake must've realized he'd thrown me off because he let out a breathy laugh, leaned forward, and planted a kiss on my forehead. "Come on." He stood and held his hand out for me to take—which I did.

I blame the alcohol.

"Don't forget the wine." Hilda stood and reached it over the table toward me, so I took it while Jake collected our glasses.

Mrs. Foster returned with a plate of cookies, and Jake had to release my hand to take them. "Thanks. These smell fantastic." He gave the room a once over. "Have a good evening, everyone. Merry Christmas."

The guests responded in kind.

"After you." Jake stepped aside so I could lead the way upstairs.

Once in our room, I stood awkwardly in the middle, clutching the merlot, while Jake set the glasses and cookies on the table beside the loveseat. He settled down on one of the cushions, then grabbed a cookie for himself. "You can join me, Laurel. I won't bite."

I stepped out of my red heels and padded across the carpet, then took a seat on the opposite end of the sofa. Jake pried the bottle from my hands and replaced it with my glass.

"Thanks," I croaked.

He laughed and his eyes crinkled in the corners. "Is being alone with me really that bad?"

I exhaled. "Sorry. I'm..."

What am I?

Confused.

Turned on.

Terrified.

"I'm a little tipsy." I brought the glass to my lips and took a hefty gulp.

Jake uncorked the bottle and refilled my goblet. "It's good to let go sometimes. Something tells me you don't do that much."

I huffed at his accurate assessment.

"I had a nice time today." He put the bottle on the table and grabbed his glass, then held it out for me. "To old friends."

"Cheers." A lump formed in my throat as I recalled how close we'd once been, and how much time I spent feeling lost without him after we'd parted ways.

He reclined against the cushion, letting his head rest on top of the back, then stretched his legs out, crossed them at the ankles, and sighed.

"Penny for your thoughts?"

"How many pennies you got?"

"As many as you need."

He blew out another breath. "Remember prom night?"

The memory hit me square in the chest. I leaned back against the cushion, mirroring his position. "Of course." It was a night I'd remember for as long as I lived. It was the first time I'd ever gotten to fall asleep nestled in his arms. We'd rented a house with our friends by one of the ski resorts for the weekend.

"You looked so unbelievably beautiful in that gold dress."

I swallowed. My twenty-eight-year-old body was gravely different from how I'd looked at eighteen.

"I didn't even care that it got glitter all over my truck. It took years to get it all out, you know," he teased.

"You're exaggerating."

"Okay, maybe not years, but it did take a long time. After you...left. Whenever I found a speck of gold glitter, it reminded me of how incredible that weekend was. Not that I needed a reminder."

I closed my eyes and remembered how perfect it had felt to make love to him in that squeaky bed with the sky-blue comforter. "Jake, that was so long ago," my voice wavered.

"It was. Yet you're still mad about something I never did."

I wet my lips and rubbed them together. My willingness to fight about that again was at a zero, so I took a deep breath and searched my heart. Despite having seen him kiss Hailey with my own eyes, something about it had never sat right with me. The Jake I'd known wouldn't have done that. Hailey, on the other hand...well, she was a conniving witch who'd never liked me and had always coveted my boyfriend. At the time, I'd been too hurt to hear reason.

But now...

"I believe you." The worlds left my mouth in a whisper.

"You do?"

I felt him lift his head and could sense him looking at me, so I opened my eyes and turned to meet his gaze. "Yes."

"Why now? Last night—"

"Last night I was stressed out and tired, and frankly a little bit—no a lotta bit—shocked by your sudden appearance."

He pushed up the sleeve of his red flannel that had unrolled. "Understandable."

"Despite what you might think, I never wanted to believe you'd cheated on me, but it's hard to reason with a heartbroken eighteen-year-old girl."

"Tell me about it." His lips curved up in one corner. "My daughter is six going on sixteen. I'm in real trouble when she hits her teen years. She inherited her mother's feistiness."

I wanted to ask him more about his ex, but the idea of Jake being with anyone other than me turned my stomach. "She's lucky to have you as her dad."

"You think?"

"Without a doubt."

Our eyes remained locked, charging the room with unspoken desire, as my heart beat loudly in my ears.

He broke away first, and cleared his throat as he fixed his gaze on his wine. "You must have a man back in the city who's worried he hasn't heard from you."

I grumbled. "Yeah, my boss."

His brows arched. "You're dating your boss?"

"Eww. No." I shook my head. "I'm not dating anyone."

He sipped his wine. "Interesting."

"How so?"

"I guess I figured you'd be married by now, what with your life plan and everything."

I'd inherited my Type A personality from my mother and had been a planner for as long as I could remember; that included a very detailed outline of how my life was going to go. Law degree by twenty-five. Married by twenty-seven. Pregnant by twenty-nine. Partner at a firm by thirty-five. While, I'd accomplished one of those things, and was on track to check off the last one, too, those middle points had proven to be pipe dreams. I ran my fingertip along the rim of my glass. "Yeah, well, life doesn't always work out as planned."

"Ain't that the truth." He clinked his glass with mine. "You're still young, though. Anything can happen."

I hemmed. "Not exactly."

"What do you mean?"

I brought the merlot to my lips for a little liquid courage before getting even more vulnerable. "My industry is cutthroat. I can't have the career *and* the family, so I had to choose."

Sadness flitted across his brow. "And you chose your career?"

"I'm good at what I do. Really good."

"I don't doubt that. I've lost plenty of arguments against you to expect anything different, counselor," he jested. "But I don't see why you can't have both."

I rested the foot of my glass on my thigh. "Manhattan is unrelenting. You either keep up or you get left behind. Having a family would put me firmly in the latter category. Besides, I work all of the time. It wouldn't be fair to whomever I dated." After an entire day off the grid, I was dreading the slew of angry messages that would be waiting for me when I got cell service back. But I had to admit, it was nice to feel like I could actually breathe for once.

Jake drummed his fingers on the cushion beside him. "Why do you do it? Don't you wish you could have both?"

"It's my career. I've worked my butt off to get to where I'm at. And, no, not really."

"That doesn't sound like the Laurel I knew."

"That's because I'm not her anymore."

"I get that, but still."

I shrugged. "It's fine. I'm fine with it. It's not like I haven't dated, it's just not for me."

"What's not for you?" His warm eyes challenged me to dive deeper into my vulnerability.

"Just forget I said anything." I downed what was left of my wine.

"No. Tell me."

I stood. "How are those cookies?" As I passed him, he

grabbed my wrist, stopping me before I could reach the end table.

"Why isn't dating for you?"

I squeezed my eyelids shut and inhaled. "Jake..."

"If you tell me, I'll tell you why I feel the same way."

My eyes snapped open and I looked down at him. "What do you mean?"

"I told you last night I haven't really dated."

I held his gaze and waited for him to finish, but he didn't. The silence hung heavy with our unspoken words. The truth lingered just under the surface, and his touch was luring it out. But I'd never even admitted it to myself. How could I admit it to him?

His lips parted.

I waited.

He inhaled.

Exhaled.

Closed his eyes.

Opened them.

Swallowed.

Finally, he broke the silence. "I haven't had any luck with dating because none of those women were you."

My stomach flipped over itself and my face grew hot as the sincerity in his gaze pleaded with me to speak my truth, too. His words unlocked a vulnerability within me, and in that moment, I felt safe. Jake had created this precious sanctuary where I could let my guard down and maybe even explore the possibility of what might've been between us once more.

"Me, too," I whispered. Confessing it out loud was like rolling a boulder off my chest. I'd spent the past decade pushing away all thoughts of Jake and had convinced myself it was because he'd hurt me, but deep down it was really because... "I've missed you."

His thumb smoothed over the back of my hand. "I've missed you, too." Without letting me go, he reached over and put his glass on the table, then took mine from me and placed it beside his. "Laurel..." his voice was low and tender as he reached for my other hand. I gave it to him, and he stood. Since I was barefoot, he towered over me, and it brought me back to our teenage years. He dipped his head to lean closer, and anticipation crackled in the gap between us. In that moment, nothing else mattered; we were cocooned away from the world, protected from the pressures of real life.

My heartrate quickened as I whispered his name. Our past, once filled with love and laughter, had been overshadowed by the pain of our separation. Yet here we were, on the brink of rekindling the connection we'd lost. *Perhaps there's a second chance for our romance after all.*

Unable to bear the distance any longer, we closed the gap. Our lips met with hesitation at first, but it quickly began to feel like coming home after a long, arduous journey, and our kiss deepened with the need to make up for lost time. Despite his facial hair scratched against my tender skin, and the fact that he tasted of red wine and sugar cookies, this kiss was unmistakably Jake. Blindfolded, I would've been able to decipher it was him. My body *knew* him. He released my hands and brought his palm up to cup the back of my neck as his tongue delved deeper into my mouth. His other hand found my hip and I stiffened. I'd never been so grateful for my shapewear before in my life.

Jake pulled back. "You okay?"

"Great."

He rested his forehead against mine and released my

neck. "I'm beginning to think that when you say something is *great*, it means the opposite." He'd always had an uncanny ability to read me. With an exhale, he grabbed my other hip, and as much as I tried to control my reaction, like a reflex, I tensed.

"I'm not...I don't..." I stammered, unable to find the words to explain my complex insecurities.

His hands ran up my rib cage, then down, over my hips, and around to my backside where he gave me a little squeeze. "I love your body."

"Don't..." I didn't need his pity or his lies.

"It's true. I told you earlier, I find you even sexier now." His hands roamed up and down my sides. "This is a woman's body. All I can think about is how fucking gorgeous you'll look bent over with my cock in you."

My skin flushed from my scalp to my toes, and my core clenched with need. Jake squeezed my right hip and at the same time his left hand slapped my behind through my chiffon wrap dress, making me squeak in surprise.

"And these," he continued as his fingertips trailed up between my breasts and settled on the bare skin of my exposed cleavage. The V-neck was why I loved that dress; it made me feel moderately attractive because my breasts were the only part of my weight gain that I liked.

Jake moaned. "I can't explain how badly I've wanted to grab these since the moment I saw you."

I stepped back, forcing his hands to fall off me. "You're being ridiculous."

His brow furrowed and his lips curved into a frown. "No, I'm not."

"Jake, no one thinks the fat girl is sexy."

He winced as though I was insulting him instead of myself. "Is that what you think? That you're *the fat girl*?"

"Don't patronize me. I'm not stupid." I held my arms out to the side and spun around so he could get a good view. "I know what I look like."

"Do you? Because if you saw what I see you wouldn't be putting yourself down like that." He held out his hand. "Come with me."

"What? Where?"

When I didn't give him my hand, he reached farther and grabbed me. "Just come." He led me into the bathroom and switched on the light, then closed the door. Hanging on the back of it was a full-length mirror. My body stiffened with nerves as he positioned me in front of the mirror and got behind me. I swallowed, not liking where this was going. I tried to avoid mirrors as much as possible.

Jake reached around and placed his hand over the bow tied at my midsection, and I sucked in my gut. With his other hand he swept my curls over my shoulder, exposing my skin, then he placed a few soft kisses where my shoulder met my neck. Chills shot through me, like they always did whenever someone touched me there. *He remembers.*

"Trust me," he whispered as his lips tenderly caressed the same spot, turning me into jelly. While his lips kept me distracted, he tugged at the bow and the forest green chiffon parted like a robe, leaving my front exposed. His hand slid over my shapewear. "You don't need this. Take it off."

"Jake, please." I straightened and tried to reach for the fabric to cover myself back up, but he was quicker. He grabbed the top and dragged my dress off my arms, letting it fall into a heap at my feet. I squirmed in an attempt to contort my body in a way that hid most of me.

"Relax, Laurel," he murmured soothingly as his fingertips danced over my arms, leaving goosebumps in their wake. "It's just me."

I closed my eyes and tried to will myself into being comfortable with this exposure.

"Would it make you feel better if I took off my clothes, too?"

I shrugged. Probably not, but I wanted to see what he had hidden under that flannel. Teenaged Jake had always been muscular and fit.

He released me long enough to work the buttons on his shirt, then he let it join my dress on the floor. Since he was behind me, I couldn't see much in the mirror, but his arms had gotten bigger—more cut—and I imagined his abs were the same. I swallowed at that realization. His effort had the opposite of the desired effect because I was even more self-conscious seeing my body in comparison, but I kept quiet. He made quick work of shedding his pants, and adding them to our pile, then he reached around me once more and found the eyehooks on the front of my mid-thigh bodysuit, at the base of my breastbone. As he released them, one-by-one, his lips on the back of my neck kept me distracted. Once he had all of the hooks undone, he slipped his fingers under the shoulder straps, and I froze at the thought of what was going to happen next.

"Can we turn off the light?" I asked.

"No. I want to see you. I want *you* to see you."

My legs began to shake with nerves.

"Trust me, sweets." His eyes met mine in the mirror and I forced myself to hold his gaze as he slid the straps off my arms. With slow and precise movements, he rolled the fabric down, pausing after my breasts sprang free. My shoulders slumped with the kind of relief that can only come from freeing your boobs from the confines of a bra.

"Gorgeous," he whispered against my ear, making the tiny hairs on the back of my neck stand up. His fingertips danced over my cleavage. "Even better than I remembered."

I was expecting him to grab my breasts, but he didn't. Instead, he got a hold of my bodysuit again and continued to roll it down. When he was just above my bellybutton, I covered his hands with mine, holding him in place. "I can't."

"You can. Your body is beautiful."

My mind flashed to my most recent sexual encounter, and how when I'd taken off my clothes, he'd been the one to reach for the bedside lamp and turn it off.

"What are you thinking?"

My chest heaved with heavy breaths, and I squeezed my eyes shut to block out the impending panic.

Jake's lips lingered by my ear. "Talk to me, sweets."

My voice trembled. "I—I don't like to look at myself." And if I didn't, why would he?

"That's a shame because I love each and every curve and dimple on your body."

My eyelids fluttered open. That was the second time Jake had used the word *love*.

"That's my girl." He grinned. "Look at me."

So, I did.

He slid his hands out from under mine and rolled the shapewear to my waist, not once breaking our eye contact, and I exhaled, feeling free of the compression that had kept me confined all day.

"I bet that's a relief," he commented before wiggling the fabric over my hips, and down my legs until the spandex joined the rest of our clothes and I was left standing there completely nude. There was something gentlemanly about the way he kept his eyes on mine instead of letting them roam my body. He slid his boxers off, and his unmistakable erection slapped against my back. "Feel what you do to me?"

I bit my lip as he grabbed my hips and pressed our bodies together.

"You haven't even touched me, and my cock is ready for you."

I arched my body, bringing us closer.

"Watch me." He brought a hand around to my throat, and I pulled my gaze away from his eyes to follow as his hand trailed down, over my right breast, just barely grazing my nipple, before doing the same to my left. With each glide of his fingertips, my anxiety shrunk and was replaced with pure desire. I stared as he continued to move down my rib cage, and over the folds of my abdomen. "So sexy," he whispered into my ear before tracing it with his tongue, almost making me forget about his hand resting on my fat.

Almost.

His fingers swiped from side to side over my pubic bone and I ached to feel him touch me where I needed him most. "Please," I uttered.

"Do you want me, too, sweets?"

I tilted my head back and rested it against his chest. There was so much to that question, but I didn't have the bandwidth to unpack it all right then, so I simply nodded.

His fingers dipped lower. Lower, Lower. Finally, they grazed over my folds, and he hummed. "So wet." He found my clit and my body jolted at the contact. "And sensitive. This is gonna be fun." His hand cupped my sex and his palm pressed against my bud as the tip of his middle finger slid into my channel. The tease had me forgetting entirely about my insecurities. All I wanted was for him to make me come. It'd been an embarrassingly long time since a guy had given me an orgasm. I hadn't had a ton of partners, but I'd been with enough to conclude that most men didn't put in the effort to fully satisfy a woman.

"Look," his voice pulled me away from my thoughts. "Watch how beautiful you are while you're being pleasured."

I lifted my head off his chest and let my gaze fall to the apex of my thighs as Jake drew circles over my clit. His pace increased, and so did the rate of my breathing as I got closer and closer.

"See how fucking sexy you are as you come apart for me. I've always loved how expressive you are."

I tried to concentrate on my reflection and the way my body writhed against his, but as my orgasm neared, I struggled to focus.

"I can feel how close you are." He slapped my clit in rapid succession, nearly catapulting me over the edge, but then he applied pressure to my tight bundle of nerves, and I was a goner. His free hand came around to cover my mouth, muffling my cries, as my body shook from the waves of pleasure coursing through me.

"That's my girl," Jake growled in my ear, and he held me as I recovered.

When I opened my eyes, I found his reflection grinning with satisfaction, and I reached behind me to grab his erection.

"We don't have to go any farther. I wanted to make you feel good. No pressure."

"I want to," I replied as my hand closed around him.

His lips parted with a breath. "Its been a while. I'm afraid I might not last too long."

"That's fine." I took my time stroking his entire length.

His jaw clenched. "I don't have any condoms."

"I'm on the pill." I needed the hormones to regulate my period thanks to stress and my weight gain.

"Are you saying I don't need one?"

I nodded as I traced the ridge around his crown.

In a swift motion, he grabbed both of my wrists and brought my hands above my head, pinning them against the mirror. "I've waited long enough to have you again." Keeping my arms pinned with one hand, he let the other drop to help guide himself to my entrance.

I rolled up onto my toes and my heart clenched as the pressure of him breaking my seal built, then released when he slid into me, and my muscles relaxed. His free hand grabbed my hip, and he took his time pumping his hips.

"Oh, Jake," I cooed as I relished in him filling me completely, then retreating.

He nibbled gently on my earlobe. "I've missed you so damn much." The emotion caught in his throat, and I realized he wasn't just talking about having sex with me.

"I've missed you, too." My mind threatened to race with the conflicting emotions of hope, fear, and vulnerability, but I swallowed them down. My crippling tendency to over-think everything could wait.

He released my hands and dug his fingers into my hips as he increased his pace. I braced myself with my arm, then reached my free hand around and threaded my fingers through the short hair covering the back of his head. I desperately needed to have him even closer, even though that wasn't really possible. Still, I tried.

His staccato breaths grew shallow signaling that he was close, and I bit the back of my forearm to keep from moaning too loudly. We were in an old house filled with people and I'd already discovered that the walls were thin.

Jake grunted. "Where do you want it?"

I thought about that, but apparently took too long because he followed that up with, "Fuck, Laurel." He pulled out and I spun, then dropped to my knees. My lips wrapped around him just in time to feel the first twitch before my mouth filled with his hot cum. I pumped him dry and swallowed. His hand smoothed over the top of my hair.

When I released him, he helped me to my feet, then pulled me into a hug. His chest was slick with sweat, but I didn't care; I held him close. Neither one of us said a word; neither one of us moved. We were cocooned in the moment —a moment we both knew wouldn't last, so we were savoring what we could.

Eventually, he stepped back and placed a kiss on my forehead. "I'll let you get cleaned up," he said as he snatched a towel off the rack and wrapped it around his waist before exiting into our bedroom.

As I used a wet cloth to clean between my legs, the overwhelming feeling of being alone hit me. It didn't matter that the only man I'd ever loved was in the adjacent room, because in a couple of days, he would go back to his life, and I would go back to mine. This evening would cease to be anything but a memory.

Once I was finished, I did my best to stretch a towel around my body because I didn't want to put my dress back on, then I took a deep breath and opened the door. Jake was laying in the bed, smiling, but when he saw me, he sat up and his smile dropped. "What's wrong?"

I shook my head as I crossed to my duffle to find clothes. "Nothing."

"You're lying."

I found my sweatshirt and pulled it over my head, then let the towel fall. "No, I'm not."

"Come here please. Stop getting dressed and lay with me."

I rubbed my lips together, then turned to face him. "We shouldn't—"

"Don't say it." The raw emotion in his voice made my heart ache. He held out his hands. "*Please*, come here."

Unable to resist him, I went over and sat beside him. "I'm here."

"Exactly." He draped his arm around me. "We're here in this moment. Don't push it away. Not yet."

I exhaled. "But, Jake, what do you think could possibly come from this besides more heartbreak?"

He squeezed my shoulder. "Regardless of what does or doesn't happen when we wake up tomorrow, I'll never regret this."

I searched for the right words to express my reservations. "I... I just don't think this was a good idea." My voice trembled, revealing the uncertainty that gripped me. "Tomorrow, we'll go to Evergreen Falls, then you'll stay there, and I'll leave."

"I know. But that doesn't mean we have to go back to being strangers. If we really wanted to make this work, we would figure it out."

I shook my head. "I don't see how."

"You don't always need a plan for everything, you know. Sometimes you have to take life one day—one minute—at a time."

I tittered. "I'm not talking about a plan. I'm simply reflecting on the facts. Your life is in Evergreen Falls, and mine is in Manhattan. You have your daughter, and I have my career."

"Okay, stop thinking like a lawyer for a minute, and tell me what you *want*. Not what's convenient, or what's challenging, just what you want."

You. That response came far too quickly for my comfort. I bit my lip.

He sighed. "If, hypothetically, there was a way we could make things work between us, would you want to try?"

I closed my eyes and summoned the courage to nod.

"Good. That's all I needed to know." He scooted us so we were laying down, and I rested my head on his bare chest, while my hand settled on his abs. "We don't have to make a single decision tonight. Let's just get some rest and enjoy being in each other's arms, okay?"

"Okay."

He kissed the top of my head, then leaned over to turn off the lamp before returning to the same position. "Good night, sweets."

"Good night," I echoed as I closed my eyes and savored the feel of Jake against me.

Like that, nestled in a random small-town inn, insulated from the real world, we drifted off to sleep.

FIVE

Jake's truck rumbled down the rural backroad that connected Whippleton with Evergreen Falls. We weren't far from home, but the drive had taken longer than we'd anticipated because the roads, while traversable, were far from good. The snow had compacted in places from other vehicles driving through, leaving behind patches of ice. I was glad Jake had convinced me to leave my car and ride with him. My Lexus most definitely would've wound up in another ditch. Jake eased off the gas as we went into a slide around a sharp turn. My heart jumped, but Jake's strong hands calmly steered us back on track. My grip on the door loosened slightly.

"I'm sorry, but you're gonna have to come to the school with me. We're cutting it close on timing," he said as he turned onto Centre Street, which ran through the main part of our village.

"That's fine. I definitely don't want you to miss your daughter's pageant," I replied. He'd been anxious all morning about getting there on time. "I'm sure my dad will be able to pick me up."

"I can drive you to your parents' after if you want to stay for the show."

"You want me to meet your daughter?" I tried not to read too much into that.

"Of course. Why wouldn't I?"

Umm because we hooked up just last night and we haven't even had a conversation about what we are yet...

We'd kept things light during the drive. It was Christmas, after all. Although, holiday or not, I didn't think either of us was too eager to have that talk. Which meant we'd come to absolutely no conclusion whatsoever about how we were going to move forward.

I must've gotten too wrapped up in my thoughts, because Jake added, "Unless you don't want to meet Adalyn."

"Sorry. Yes, I would love to meet her." That was true. This little girl was a part of Jake, and I'd loved him once.

I gazed through the window at all the shops decked out for the holiday, including my parents' diner and Jake's hardware store. The decor wasn't as elaborate (or expensive) as some of the window displays in the city, but there was a nostalgia about these that sort of made them better. Up ahead, the towering evergreen tree, covered in lights and giant ornaments, sat in the middle of the Village Square. Seeing that brought a sense of peace to my edgy nerves.

Jake turned right and the elementary school came into view. I grinned at the sight of kids sledding on the same hill we'd grown up playing on. "Wow, this is really taking me back."

Jake followed where I was looking. "That'll always be the best sledding hill."

The tradition hadn't ended with our childhood. As

teens, Jake and I still went down that hill. "Sure is. Remember senior year—"

"How could I forget?" Jake chuckled. "I seem to recall a certain someone using my inner tube as a crash pad."

"Hey, you lived didn't you?" I teased.

Jake gave me his crooked smile. I'd always loved that. He pulled into the parking lot, which was filled with pickups and snowmobiles. "What time is it?" he asked as he looped around to find a spot. The electronics in his truck's dashboard were on the fritz from the cold.

I slipped my gloved hand into the pocket of my coat and retrieved my phone. "Two minutes past ten."

"Shit."

"It's okay. We're here. I bet these things don't even start on time. They've got a lot of young kids to coordinate."

"Yeah, you're right."

My screen lit up with notifications. I'd silenced it to avoid a barrage of dings once I regained service. The number of missed calls and emails from Alan was staggering. But, that was a future-me problem. As Jake parked, I returned the device to my pocket. The only thing I needed to focus on for the next hour was *The Story of Christmas*, as performed by a bunch of little kids.

We hurried inside and made a beeline for the auditorium. The lights were off and one of the teachers was making an announcement about no flash photography. Jake stopped at the first set of empty seats and gestured for me to go first, then he plopped himself down in the aisle.

Immediately following the announcement, a group of kindergartners came out dressed as elves and gingerbread men. They sang an off-key version of "Jingle Bells," but it was so cute, no one cared how it sounded. Watching all this unfold, I couldn't help but reminisce about my own childhood Christmas pageants. The faulty costumes, forgotten lines, and post-show sugar highs. Evergreen Falls felt suspended in time. There was something comforting about that reliability.

One little girl tripped over her too-big elf shoes, and the audience erupted into sympathetic laughter. Next year, my niece would be up there. I made a promise to myself then that I wouldn't miss it. These moments were too important. I eyed Jake in my periphery. He was watching the kids with a tender expression, and I could tell he was picturing Adalyn up there. My heart stirred, flooded by a longing I hadn't felt in years. Before I could try and process that, the kindergarteners finished their number and scampered off stage.

"She's next," he whispered as he wiggled in his seat. The sheer excitement he had over seeing his little girl threatened to bring tears to my eyes. The first graders were reenacting the nativity story, complete with makeshift costumes thrown together from stuff found in the townspeople's closets. It didn't take long for Adalyn to make her debut as the Virgin Mary, and I didn't need the costume to tell me she was Jake's daughter; she was a spitting image of him. Plus, Jake made a scene clapping and cheering for her when she entered. A giant smile stretched across the little girl's face when she spotted her dad in the crowd, and she gave him a covert wave. The pride etched in his expression stirred up a cacophony of emotions within me. My mind wandered to the what ifs of the life we could've shared. Had things not fallen so spectacularly to pieces ten years ago, would we be there watching *our* daughter on that stage? I blew out a breath.

Without taking his eyes off that stage, Jake's hand covered mine and squeezed. I wondered what he was thinking. Was he imagining a future where doing things like this together was normal for us? Because if so, he was going to end up with a broken heart. Again. If I learned one thing from watching Jake with his daughter, it was that he was never going to leave Evergreen Falls—nor would I want him to. His daughter needed him there.

The crowd chuckled, drawing me out of my head. One boy was hamming it up as a shepherd. As the segment progressed, another girl kept forgetting her single line as an angel and had to be prompted by the teacher offstage, but the audience remained patient and encouraging. As for Adalyn, she remembered all her lines perfectly. She was a natural born performer. Clearly, she inherited her dad's charisma.

For the big finale, the narrator announced the birth of Jesus, and Adalyn bent forward in her chair, reached through her dress and retrieved the baby doll that'd been hidden under her chair, then she plopped it down on her lap. Her earnestness had the audience roaring, and I caught Jake wiping a tear from his eye. Yes, he was precisely the kind of man I would want to have a family with—if I ever changed my mind on that, that is.

As the first graders took their bows, Jake released my hand and got to his feet. He cheered louder than anyone when it was Adalyn's turn to have her moment in the spotlight. I scanned the audience and wondered where Adalyn's mother was. There was a blond woman one section over from ours and a few rows up who seemed to cheer extra enthusiastically, but I didn't get a good look at her. Once the stage was cleared, we returned to our seats.

"She did great," I whispered.

Jake turned toward me with the biggest grin. "She did, didn't she?"

"You have a talented little girl."

"Thanks." His eyes locked with mine, and the air between us began to charge.

"Next up, our second-grade class will perform 'Santa's Workshop.'" The principal returned to the microphone, breaking up our moment. It was probably for the best.

The second graders shuffled out in their makeshift elf costumes. The music started and the kids began singing a cheerful tune about Santa's workshop at the North Pole. Jake reached for my hand again, and he held it until the end of the pageant. When it was over, Jake gave my hand a little squeeze. "I better go get Adalyn. Wanna come with me?"

I hesitated. Despite what he'd said in the car, meeting his daughter felt like a big step, and I wasn't sure I was ready for it. But before I could respond, he was already standing up and motioning for me to follow him. We made our way through the crowded aisles to the side of the stage. A woman with a clipboard checked Jake's name against a list and then pointed us toward the back. When we got up the steps, kids ran around in all directions, chattering excitedly with their families.

"Daddy!" Adalyn shouted when she spotted Jake, and she came running, flinging herself into his arms.

He scooped her up and spun her around. "You were amazing, baby girl," he said, planting a kiss on her cheek. "The best one up there."

"My teacher said I did the goodest," she bragged as Jake placed her back on the ground. She was still wearing her costume, which up close looked to be like an oversized blue T-shirt, with a white pillowcase artfully pinned over her head.

Adalyn's eyes drifted to me. "Who's that?"

Jake motioned for me to come forward. "This is my friend Laurel. She used to live here too, a long time ago."

The girl gave me a dimpled smile. "Hi! I'm Adalyn."

"It's very nice to meet you, Adalyn." I couldn't get over how much she looked like Jake—same eyes, nose, even his crooked grin. "You did a wonderful job today."

She radiated pride. "Thanks. Daddy practiced with me a lot."

"And you nailed it, just like I said you would." Jake put his hand out for her to high five.

Adalyn turned back to me, curiosity glinting in her eyes. "Do you have any kids in the pageant?"

"Oh...uh, no I don't."

Her face fell a little. "How come? They don't go to school here?"

I chuckled awkwardly. "No. I don't have kids. But my niece is going to start kindergarten here next year."

She perked up. "She'll get to be in the pageant then, too."

"Yes, she will."

Jake shot me an apologetic look, but I just smiled. Adalyn's innocence was endearing. He rescued me from his daughter's inquisition by saying, "Everyone is here to see you, so we should go say hi."

"Yay," she cheered as she turned and started to run toward the exit.

Jake shook his head and laughed. "I told you. Six going on sixteen."

I nudged his arm. "Yeah, but you've got this. Being a dad suits you." When his daughter disappeared from view, I added, "Umm, shouldn't you run up and get her."

"She knows where to go," he replied, a little too laidback for my liking.

I'd just met the kid and my heart was going haywire over not seeing her. "You're not worried she'll get kidnapped."

He squeezed my shoulder. "You've definitely been in the city too long. This is Evergreen Falls where no one locks their doors and the only crime we see is teenagers getting high under the bleachers. If you even want to call that a crime."

"Right." I exhaled. Being a lawyer often made me assume the worst about humanity; I hated that.

"Although we did have an incident last summer where someone ripped up Mrs. Granger's prize-winning sunflowers. It was a real scandal."

I let out a laugh. "Point taken."

As we returned to the theater, I couldn't help but notice multiple people watching us. Some of whom I recognized, others not. Jake must've picked up on it, too, because he said, "Us being here together will feed the rumor mill for a little while."

I'd gotten so used to being invisible in Manhattan that I'd nearly forgotten what it was like to be in a small town where everyone knew everyone else's business. I glanced in the direction Adalyn had run off in and saw Jake's family approaching. My nerves got the best of me, and I paused. "I'm going to run to the restroom."

He eyed me quizzically, but thankfully didn't press. "Sure. We'll be around here somewhere."

"Great." I turned and headed in the opposite direction. Meeting Jake's daughter had been enough for one day, I wasn't up for a full Hansen family reunion, too. I weaved through the crowd but hadn't gotten too far when a familiar voice piped up behind me. "Laurel Mercer? Is that you?"

I turned to see Percival Winslow hurrying over,

decked out in full Victorian garb, complete with top hat and cane. He was Evergreen Falls' eccentric local historian who took his role very seriously, especially this time of year.

"Hi, Percival. Merry Christmas."

"Merry Christmas to you, as well." He peered at me through his little round spectacles. "My word, its been ages. What brings you back to our fine village?"

"I came to visit my family for the holiday."

"Ahh, yes. Good people you Mercers. You know, back in the day, your grandfather and I worked on the same farm."

Before I could explain that he'd told me the story many times, he launched into one of his long-winded spiels about how that farm factored into the town's history, the founding families, and so on. I didn't really mind. It was just his way. As Percival rambled on, I glanced over his shoulder at Jake. He was standing beside his mother who had her arms wrapped around Adalyn. The image made my heart squeeze. I'd always liked Jake's mom and could imagine her being a fantastic grandma.

Then I noticed a blond approaching their group, and I wondered if it was the woman in the audience whom I had suspected of being Adalyn's mother. Her back was to me as she leaned in and gave Jake a quick hug, then she turned, and I stiffened.

Hailey Jennings.

Seeing her so close to Jake made me want to launch myself across the room and tackle her. I was too far away to hear, but Hailey said something that made Adalyn turn. The little girl's face lit up and she reached for Hailey who took her with far too much familiarity. I didn't need anyone to tell me that the evil witch who'd ruined my life was the mother of Jake's child.

My blood sank to my feet and an overwhelming wave of nausea made me sway.

Percival eyed me with concern. "Is something wrong?"

I couldn't trust myself to speak without vomiting. The betrayal had me lightheaded as I flashed back to that day ten years ago when I'd caught the two of them kissing. It had nearly destroyed me, yet somehow this felt worse.

It was so stupid of me to trust Jake when he'd insisted that he hadn't cheated on me with *her*. Plus, we'd spent a whole day and a half together and not once had it dawned on him to tell me that he fathered a child with that c-u-next-tuesday?! My whole head turned hot, threatening to boil my brain.

Percival followed my gaze. "Oh, my." He faced me once more with understanding in his wrinkled expression. "Come now, let's get you home," he said gently, taking my arm.

I didn't argue as he led me outside. In fact, for once I was grateful that I was in a town where everyone knew my business because that meant I didn't have to explain why I suddenly looked like I'd seen a ghost. No, a demon. The devil herself. On freaking Christmas.

"My car is this way," Percival gestured to the right.

"I just need to get my bags." I pointed towards Jake's truck and hoped that he'd been earnest when he'd mentioned not using locks. Lucky for me, that was one thing he hadn't lied to me about. The door opened with ease, and I retrieved my things, hating how they smelled of sawdust—like *him*—then I stomped through the snow to Percival's waiting vehicle. It was a black pickup, decorated to resemble an old horse drawn carriage. An hour ago, I would've found it festive and fun, but now...

I wanted to eradicate any holiday joy.

I never should've come home for Christmas.

SIX

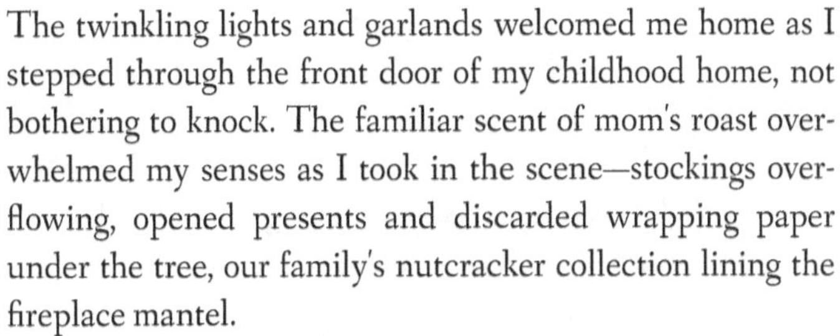

The twinkling lights and garlands welcomed me home as I stepped through the front door of my childhood home, not bothering to knock. The familiar scent of mom's roast overwhelmed my senses as I took in the scene—stockings overflowing, opened presents and discarded wrapping paper under the tree, our family's nutcracker collection lining the fireplace mantel.

After dropping my bags by the door, I meandered down the hall to the dining room, then poked my head in. "Do you have room for one more?"

Mom squealed as she dropped her fork and ran toward me, enveloping me in a hug. It was exactly what I needed after the morning I'd endured.

"Laurel, what are you doing here?" she pulled away to ask before dragging me back in for another hug.

"I thought I'd surprise you all for Christmas."

Mom's eyes glistened with happy tears. "This is the greatest Christmas gift."

"Give someone else a turn, Justine," my dad's deep voice carried from over Mom's shoulder. She stepped aside and he filled her absence. "Welcome home," he said as he embraced me and pressed a kiss to my forehead. "Christmas hasn't been the same without you."

I hadn't been home for the holidays in eight years, and having this moment made me sorely regret that.

When Dad let go, Aspen threw her arms around me. "Hey, sis."

I squeezed my eyes closed and swallowed. Their affection was precisely the balm I needed, and I fought to keep my emotions in check. My sister released me and my brother-in-law, Danny, stepped up, holding my two-year-old nephew Lyle.

"Look how big you've gotten," I said as I tickled the Santa face on his t-shirt, making him giggle.

Danny wrapped one arm around me and patted my back. "Good to see you."

"You, too." Even though he'd grown up in Evergreen Falls, he and Aspen hadn't started dating until after I'd left. "I'm glad to see you got the day off," I remarked.

"Sort of. I work tonight. That's why we're eating so early." He was one of the four deputies Evergreen Falls had.

Aspen urged my four-year-old niece forward. She was being shy and hiding behind her mom. "Say hi to Aunt Laurel, Gemma."

She raised her little hand, then immediately returned to clutching Aspen's pant leg.

My sister patted my niece's head. "Give her a little time. She'll warm up."

"It's fine," I replied, as though it didn't sting. But I couldn't blame her. I was basically a stranger she saw once a year. "Hi, Grampy," I said as I worked my way around the table to where he was sitting in his wheelchair. I leaned over and gave him a hug.

"I would get up to greet you properly, but the wheel-chair police will have me arrested," he grumbled as he gestured to my parents. "How are you doing, kiddo?"

"I'm great," I replied. Choosing not to mention how over-worked and burnt out I was, I opted to go with, "Work has me busy now that I'm a senior associate." That reminded me of the mountain of notifications I had to attend to, and I stiffened.

"Sit down and make a plate," my dad said as he handed me a clean one from the China closet. "I'll go get your bags out of the car."

"Uh, about that." I sat beside Grampy and speared a few slices of the roast. "I don't have my car."

My dad's thick brows furrowed. "How'd you get here?" There weren't exactly public transportation options in the middle of nowhere.

As I scooped some mashed potatoes onto my plate, I contemplated how to explain the situation without bringing Jake into things. I wasn't prepared to talk about him. I'd been embarrassed enough when he'd kissed Hailey before, I didn't think I could handle that humiliation again. "Well, I drove most of the way here, but I got caught in the blizzard—"

"Wait, that was the other night," my dad interjected.

I ladled some gravy over my plate. "Right. I would've been here sooner, but a deer ran me into a drainage ditch."

Mom clutched her chest. "Are you okay? Do you need to see a doctor?"

"I'm fine." I cut off a piece of the meat. "So is my car...I think. It's just stuck."

"Why didn't you call me?" Dad asked. "I would've come and gotten you."

"No cell service, so I had to wait for someone to drive by.

I spent the night at a b and b, where I was snowed in all day yesterday until I was able to get a ride here."

"Oh, honey," Mom lamented. "That sounds like quite the ordeal."

You have no idea. I savored a bite of the tender beef.

"Where's your car?" my brother-in-law asked.

"Somewhere by Whippleton. It was dark and visibility was too poor to get a precise location."

Danny bounced Lyle on his knee. "If you give me your keys, I'll take a ride out there with one of the guys tonight and see if we can get it."

"Thank you. That's so sweet of you."

"It's nothing."

"Well, I really appreciate it. I've got a trial coming up in a few days, so I'm going to have to leave tomorrow."

"So soon?" My mom's whole demeanor saddened, and it hit me square in the gut. "But you just got here."

"The girl is busy, Justine," Grampy chimed in.

"I know, but we don't get to see her very often. Can't you stay a little while longer?" she pleaded.

"There are a few things I need to attend to today after we eat, so let me see what I can get done. Maybe I can leave Sunday instead."

"You have work to do on Christmas?" Aspen asked, then she held out her palm and shook her head. "Never mind. I forgot who I was talking to for a second."

"What does that mean?"

She shook her head. "It's nothing. Just that I know how dedicated you are to your career."

I squinted in her direction. "I'm here, aren't I?"

"You are."

"Aspen," Mom snapped. "It's Christmas."

She tossed up her hands. "What'd I do?"

I pushed my plate back. "If I don't do my job, then an innocent man will be spending New Years in prison instead of at home with his pregnant wife."

"That's enough, girls," Dad scolded in the commanding tone he'd used on us quite often at that very table.

Aspen sighed. "I didn't mean anything by it. I get that you have an important job."

"It's okay." I stood up from the table. "I need to catch up on work since I didn't have internet access all day yesterday. I'll be back down in a bit."

My mom shot Aspen an irritated look before turning to me with a sympathetic smile. "Of course, sweetheart. Let me know if you need anything."

I nodded and headed upstairs to my old bedroom, which looked exactly the same as when I'd left for college ten years ago, right down to the boy band posters on the wall. After changing into comfier clothes, I curled up on the bed and pulled out my phone, scrolling through the angry messages from Alan, threatening my job. There were also texts from Jake.

Jake: Hey where'd you go?

Jake: Someone said you left with Percival Winslow. I would've given you a ride.

Jake: I see you got your bags. Enjoy dinner with your family. Talk later?

Deciding to ignore those, I tossed my cell onto the mattress and flipped open my laptop to get started on my emails. It was much easier to deal with my irrational, hot-headed boss than it was to confront Jake about what he'd done.

A short while later, a soft knock at the door pulled me away from the reply I was typing. "Come in," I called.

My mom entered with two mugs of hot chocolate, just like she used to bring me as a kid whenever I was upset. "Thought you could use this."

"Thanks, Mom." I grabbed a mug as she sat down beside me.

"Don't take what Aspen said to heart," she said gently. "We're just happy you're here."

"I know. It's just..." I stared down at the marshmallows melting into the chocolate. "Well, she isn't wrong. All I do is work."

"You certainly are dedicated. Always have been, even as a young girl. You were always the first to sign up for extra shifts at the diner." She brushed a strand of hair from my face. "But take it from someone who knows—don't let your career take over your life. Make time for the people you love, too."

"I know, Mom," I said softly before blowing into the hot mug. "I'm trying."

She gave me a warm smile that reminded me of the photo of her I had on my desk at work. "That's all you can do. Thank you for coming for Christmas."

"Of course." I took a sip of the sweet, creamy hot choco-late, letting it warm me from the inside out. It tasted like childhood—like simpler times when juggling a demanding career and staving off heartbreak weren't anywhere on my radar.

There was another knock on my door. I exhaled. "Come in."

Aspen poked her head in. "If I'm interrupting, I can come back."

"Not at all." Mom stood. "I'll leave you to it. I'm going to enlist Gemma to help me with the cookies."

As Mom passed her, Aspen said, "Don't let her eat too much, please."

"I'll try." Mom closed the door behind her.

Aspen sighed. "She isn't going to try at all. I swear, that woman never let either one of us get away with the things she lets my kids do."

"I hear that's how grandparents are." I tucked one leg underneath me as I recalled how ours had spoiled us.

Aspen took a few tentative steps toward me. "About before, I'm sorry."

"We're all good. Don't worry about it."

She pointed at my bed. "Can I?"

"Sure."

She took a seat on the edge. "I really am glad to see you. It's not the same around here without my big sister."

I gave her a wistful nod. "I miss you, too. The kids are so big. I hardly even recognize them."

"Six months is a long time at their age. Developmentally."

I traced the rim of my mug with my fingertip. "I wish I could be around more. I hate that I'm missing them grow up."

"I wish you could be, too. I know Mom and Dad would love it."

I rubbed my lips together. "I could help out with Grampy, also. I really hate seeing him in that chair. When we were kids, he always seemed so invincible."

Aspen crossed one leg over the other. "Tell me about it.

It frustrates him a lot. Mom and Dad are trying their best, but you know how stubborn Grampy can be."

I snorted. That trait certainly ran in our family.

"The thing is though, he really can't walk very far, so I don't know why he even wants to try."

"I think it's more about him refusing to come to terms with losing some of his independence."

My sister's head drooped. "That I can understand."

I scooted closer. "Why do I feel like we're not talking about Grampy anymore..."

Her shoulders slumped with a sigh.

"What's wrong, Aspen?"

Her lip began to quiver, so she bit it. "Don't get me wrong, I love my kids more than anything."

"Of course, you do." I wrapped an arm around her back.

"I just feel like, I don't know, all I am is a mom."

"What do you mean?"

"I help out at the diner when I can, but other than that, all of my time is taken up by my children."

While our circumstances were different—opposite even —I definitely understood her desire for more in life. "There's nothing wrong with you wanting to do something for yourself."

Aspen had always been content working at our family diner. She didn't go to college, and she married Danny when she was twenty, then they had Gemma a year later. My sister never had the opportunity to explore her own interests like I had.

She blew out a breath. "What would I do though?"

"Anything you want."

"Come on, Laur, you know as well as I do that options are slim in Evergreen Falls. This is nothing like Manhattan."

"Trust me, things in the city aren't all that great either.

With the internet today though, there are plenty of remote opportunities if you want to find a job."

She stretched her neck from side-to-side. "Forget I mentioned it. It's not like I'll have any time for a job at least until Lyle starts school in three years."

I hated that I couldn't be around to help her. Not that I knew what I could do, but at the very least I could babysit.

She flashed me a mischievous grin. "Word going around is that you were at the elementary school Christmas pageant this morning with Jake Hansen."

The abrupt subject change about gave me whiplash. I sputtered, "I—uh—wow. That didn't take long."

"Welcome home." She nudged me in the side. "Care to explain?"

I avoided her gaze, tucking a lock of hair behind my ear. "There isn't much to explain," I lied. "He happened to be passing by the other night when I was stranded in a ditch, so he gave me a ride."

"Mmm hmm," Aspen said knowingly. "Now is probably a good time for me to tell you that Jake and Danny are good friends."

"What? They are?"

"Yeah. Ever since Danny joined the fire department a couple of years ago."

I cocked my head. "You never told me that."

"Yeah, well, you made it clear a long time ago that you never wanted to so much as hear the name Jake Hansen ever again."

She had me there. I fiddled with the hem of my sweatshirt.

"So, is there anything else you'd like to add?"

I sighed, knowing I couldn't hide anything from my

sister. "It's complicated, okay? I don't really want to talk about it."

She nodded understandingly and squeezed my hand. "Okay. But whenever you're ready, I'm here."

I smiled gratefully and the knot in my chest loosened. "Thank you."

"Of course. Family first."

"Family first," I echoed, even though I'd done a lousy job of upholding that sentiment. But that was about to change. I wasn't sure how, but if I'd learned anything from this trip, it was that Evergreen Falls was my home, and it always would be.

SEVEN

The twinkling, multi-colored lights draped around the towering evergreen in the center of the village square cast a magical glow, as if transported from the pages of a story-book. The crisp, pine-scented air carried notes of roasted chestnuts and cinnamon buns from the vendor stalls, reminding me of the city, but so much better. Children's laughter mingled with the chorus of carolers filling the square with festive melodies. It was a long-standing tradition for the town to congregate in the Village Square on Christmas night and sing holiday classics.

I soaked in the nostalgic scene with my niece, Gemma, pressed against my side, smiling up at me. Her shyness from earlier had vanished after I'd played tea party with her that afternoon using the new set that Santa had brought her. Now she clung to me as if I'd always been her best friend. The familiar lyrics of "Deck the Halls" rose in the air as we joined voices with our neighbors. Despite not knowing the words, Gemma shouted at the top of her lungs, "Ducks and dolls with bows and lollies," followed by an incoherent stream of *la-la-las*. It made me laugh so hard I could barely sing.

Through her own laughter, Aspen leaned over and said, "At least she has enthusiasm."

"I kind of like her lyrics better."

I glanced at my family lined up around the tree. Dad had his arm around my mother, and they swayed in unison. Thirty-three years of marriage, and they were still crazy about each other. My little nephew stood on his great-grandpa's legs and wiggled his diapered behind while Grampy held his tiny hands. In welcome contrast to the stress earlier that day, this moment brought me immense solace. The rich and spicy scent of pine filled each breath I took, transporting me back to childhood nights like this— back to a time when dreams still lay ahead, untouched by life's unexpected twists and turns.

Gemma squeezed my hand, drawing me back. "Look, Aunt Laurel. Daddy truck." She pointed excitedly at the fire engine that had pulled up and was parking at the edge of the grass.

"Daddy is working his other job tonight, baby," Aspen said.

The little girl's shoulder slumped. "Oh."

Hating to see her tiny spirit shatter, I suggested, "Why don't we go take a look at the truck anyway?"

"Yay, yay, yay, yay," she chanted while jumping up and down.

Aspen lowered her voice so only I would hear. "You know Jake is a lieutenant, right?"

I nodded. "Surely, he's with his daughter tonight, though." Especially since he'd missed spending Christmas Eve with her.

"Come onnnn." Gemma tugged on my hand, so I went with her to see the engine.

"When I was your age, Gramps used to take me to the firehouse to see the trucks all the time."

"Mommy and Daddy, too?"

I wasn't equipped to explain how mommies and daddies came from different families, so I simply replied, "Yes."

"My daddy is catching bad guys tonight," she sing-songed with pride as she skipped toward the giant red truck, which was decked out with wreaths.

The passenger side door opened and out dropped the very last person I wanted to see. It stopped me in my tracks.

Gemma eyed me quizzically as she pulled on my hand. "Truck," was all she said, and being that I wasn't about to disappoint her, I inhaled deeply and shook off my nerves. If I was going to be spending any kind of time in Evergreen Falls in the future, I'd have to get used to the idea of seeing Jake eventually.

As badly as I wanted to look away, I found myself staring at him. He was looking unfairly cute in a Santa hat and his turnout gear, as he handed candy canes to the swarm of kids.

In a moment of distraction, Gemma managed to wiggle free from my grasp and she charged toward the truck, shouting, "Uncle Jake."

Well, isn't that freaking fantastic. My niece calls him uncle.

"Gemma," I hollered. "Careful."

At the sound of my voice, Jake turned my way and waved, right before Gemma attacked his legs. He gave her a hug and it made me equal parts swoony and mad. After everything he'd done, he didn't deserve access to *my* family.

It took every ounce of courage I had to keep walking that way.

"Hey," he said when I got within earshot. "I've been trying to reach you."

Ignoring him I held my hand out for Gemma. "How about we go get some cocoa?"

She held up her candy cane. "Open."

"Please?" I urged as I took it from her.

"Pwease."

I bit off the tip of the plastic, then peeled it back, and handed it to her.

"Thank you." She put the candy in her mouth.

"Laurel?"

I angled my body away, pretending not to hear him. I wasn't about to get into it with him in front of my niece. Gemma's little eyes darted from me to Jake. That was when I realized she was entirely too smart for her age. Not wanting her to sense the tension, I plastered on a grin. "Come on, sweetie. Let's get cocoa to go with that candy cane." I tried to get her to take my hand again.

Rooted to her spot, she pointed up at the engine. The door to the rear cab was open and children were taking turns sitting in the seats.

"You can check it out," Jake said as he lifted Gemma up effortlessly. Seeing Jake's natural ease with kids about made my ovaries cry.

"Careful with the candy. No jumping around," I shouted so she would hear me.

Jake tucked his hands into the pocket of his coat. "You're mad."

With raised brows and parted lips, I gave him a look that hopefully made him feel stupid for having made such an obvious statement.

Just then, Aspen appeared. "Hey, everything okay?"

I gave her a curt nod.

She leaned close and whispered, "You sure?"

I blew out a breath and tried to let some of the anger dissipate. "Yeah. Thanks."

"Okay." She glanced at Jake. "Hey."

"Hi, Aspen." He pointed toward the truck. "Gemma's in there."

"Thanks." My sister turned her attention to her daughter, but stayed close to me and I could tell she was listening and waiting for me to say I needed rescuing.

"Can we go somewhere and talk?" Jake asked.

Truthfully, the last thing I wanted to do was hear whatever lie he was going to tell me next, but there was also a part of me that felt I deserved answers, so I sighed and said, "Fine."

Jake placed a hand on Aspen's shoulder. "Adalyn's back there. Can you keep an eye on her for me?"

My sister nodded. "Sure."

"Thanks." He tucked his hands back into his coat pockets. "This way."

I followed him around the gazebo and when we found an empty bench that wasn't surrounded by people, he gestured for me to sit, but I remained standing. He ran a hand over his beard and made the first move, taking a seat on the cold wood. I tugged my knit hat over my ears, then conceded and sat at the opposite end. I waited, arms crossed, as Jake seemed to struggle to find the right words.

"I take it you know," he finally said.

"Know what?" I played dumb.

He blew out a breath. "I'm sorry I didn't tell you about Hailey. I could've handled that better."

My jaw tightened. "No kidding."

He grimaced. "It's not what you think?"

"Oh, really?" I shook my head in disbelief. "Just last night you were begging me to believe that you didn't cheat on me with her, meanwhile you have a child together."

"I swear to you, I *never* cheated on you, Laurel."

I snickered. "Fool me once shame on you. Fool me twice shame on me. There won't be a third time, Jake." I stood to leave, but he grabbed my arm.

"Can you just hear me out?" he pleaded, his expression stricken.

Despite my better judgment. I lowered back onto the bench.

"Thank you." He swallowed. "Everything I said about that night of the party was true. You can ask Hailey yourself."

I snorted. "Hard pass." Next to Jake, Hailey Jennings was the very last human being on the planet I wanted to speak to.

"Fine. Ask anyone. Hailey admitted what she did a long time ago."

I crossed my legs and bounced my foot, wishing this conversation was over. "Okay, whatever you say. You didn't cheat," I placated him. "That doesn't explain how you two...." I trailed off, the thought of Jake and Hailey dating and having sex was too nauseating to finish.

Jake dragged a hand down his face. "It was one time, years ago. I was at the bar drinking..." He hung his head. "There was really no other reason other than that she was there. I made a stupid mistake, and I regretted it immediately."

My stomach somersaulted at the image threatening to play out in my mind. "Hailey? Of all people? If—and this is a big if—what you're saying about the night of the party is true, then she caused our breakup. Not to mention the torture she put me through in high school. She's pure evil. I don't understand how you could..." I flicked my wrist. "Ugh."

"I'm not gonna defend what she did back then, but we were teenagers. Hailey has grown up a lot. She's not so bad."

I coughed. He might as well have driven an ice pick through my heart. "Not so bad? She broke us up, Jake. Do you seriously forgive her for that?"

He scratched at his beard. "For my daughter's sake, I've moved passed that. I had to."

I wanted to be mad at him for that, but I couldn't. A child was involved. "Speaking of your daughter, I'm confused. Why invite me to the Christmas Pageant? You had to know I would see Hailey. Do you really have such little respect for me that ambushing me with the truth was your best option?"

He reached a hand out to touch my thigh, then thought better of it when I glared and retreated. "She was supposed to be in Niagara Falls with her boyfriend for Christmas, but they canceled because of the storm. I had no idea, or I absolutely would've told you beforehand. The last thing I wanted was for you to feel ambushed, Laurel."

I searched his face, looking for any hint of deception, but found only earnestness. My shoulders dropped a fraction. "Okay, fine. But why didn't you tell me when we were in Whippleton? You had plenty of chances to come clean about Hailey." Her name left such a foul taste in my mouth.

He looked down at his lap. "I don't know. I guess I panicked. I thought if you knew about her you'd..."

"I'd what?"

He met my gaze again. "Look at me with the hatred that's in your eyes now."

I let out a long breath. "I don't hate you." Despite our

complicated history, one thing I could never bring myself to do was hate him.

"At the very least you're disappointed."

"Valid."

"I'm really sorry, Laurel," Jake said softly. "Truly. The last thing I wanted was to hurt you again."

My heart constricted at the regret in his voice. It seemed I wasn't the only one haunted by the past. I swallowed. "I need some time to...process."

"Of course. Take all the time you need. I'll be here."

Our eyes locked and I had to force myself to break the trance. Needing some space to reflect after that emotional conversation before rejoining my family, I made my way over to the hot cocoa stand. As I waited in line, blowing into my gloves to warm my frozen fingers, someone tapped my shoulder, and I turned.

"Hi, Percival." I tried to shake off my foul mood and smile.

"It is indeed lovely to see you out and about."

"I couldn't miss caroling in the square. It's a tradition."

"It 'tis, it 'tis." He adjusted his monocle. "It all started back in nineteen-eleven when—"

"Excuse me." An older gentleman who looked familiar, but whose name I couldn't place joined our circle. "I'm sorry to interrupt, but are you Laurel Mercer?"

"I am."

"Splendid. I was having a chat with your mother, and she suggested that you and I talk. Do you have a minute?"

I glanced at Percival, who must've picked up on my uncertainty because he said, "Oh, yes, Roger. As Evergreen Falls' resident attorney, you and Ms. Mercer will have plenty to talk about."

Recognition dawned, and I was grateful for Percival's

astute interjection. Roger Boone had aged significantly since I'd last seen him. *When was that?* It had to have been when I was still in high school.

Percival excused himself, leaving me to speak with Roger.

"How are you, Mr. Boone?" I asked as we moved up in the line.

"Truth be told, I'm getting tired. Don't get old," he jested. "Your mom tells me you're a senior associate at a defense law firm in Manhattan."

"I am." Typically I wouldn't have minded talking about my career with the town lawyer, but after everything with Jake, I wasn't up for small talk.

"That's quite impressive at your age. How do you like it?"

"Can't complain," I replied politely. Then, before I realized what had overcome me, I added, "Actually, I'm tired, too, Mr. Boone." Not only was I flat out exhausted from work, but I was also tired of pretending like I wasn't.

He studied me for a moment, perceptive as always. "Our profession doesn't necessarily have to be that demanding, you know."

I shrugged as we stepped closer to the front of the line. "I'm paying my dues."

The older man adjusted the knit scarf—clearly handmade, most likely by his wife. "I'll cut to the chase. Lately, I've been thinking it's about time I retire. These old bones just aren't what they used to be. Been looking for someone to take over my practice here in town, but there are no other lawyers in Evergreen Falls."

I stared at him. "Wait...are you offering me a job?"

"Sort of," he chuckled. "I'm offering you the opportunity to take over my practice."

"Wow." My mind reeled as I stepped up to the counter and ordered two hot chocolates, buying myself a minute to think. His offer had caught me completely off guard. I tried to picture myself with my own practice in Evergreen Falls. It was a chance to move back home, and to be near my family again.

But I had a life in New York, and a career I'd worked hard for. His offer, while tempting, conflicted with the future I'd envisioned for myself. Then again, I'd been starting to question that plan.

The teenager behind the counter took my money and handed me the two cups. I gave one to Mr. Boone.

"Oh, thank you."

"You're welcome."

We stepped away from the counter and stood off to the side. "I appreciate your offer, and I'm honored that you're even considering me, but do you mind if I take some time to mull it over?"

"Of course, dear. You know where to find me." He patted my shoulder. "Merry Christmas."

"Merry Christmas," I returned.

As I meandered through the crowd of carolers, I imagined what life would be like calling these people my neighbors again. I cradled my paper cup, letting the cocoa warm my numb fingers, as I came to a stop beside the towering evergreen that served as the centerpiece of our village. I let out a long exhale, my breath fogging the air, as I tried to wrap my head around it all. Both Mr. Boone's offer and my talk with Jake had left me feeling off-kilter. For the first time, I seriously questioned the path I was on, and I feared the answer that I so desperately wished would drop magically from the sky, wasn't going to be so simple to come by.

EIGHT

SIX DAYS LATER

The tape ripped off the last box with a satisfying zip, freeing the contents of my old life. I sank onto the bare mattress, gazing around my new home. The sleek furniture and modern art that had filled my living space in the city, seemed vastly out of place in the quaint one-bedroom apartment above my parents' diner. It was temporary until I could find a more fitting location, but it worked fine for the time being. The important thing was that I was officially back in Evergreen Falls, the little town I'd left behind a decade ago. My skyscraper view had been replaced by rolling hills and snow-capped mountains that I had adored as a child.

After I'd returned to Manhattan from my Christmas break, I'd forced myself to push aside the options that had been presented to me during my visit home, and I focused on my case. After winning the trial for my client's freedom, the choice had become clear. I'd expected to feel an overwhelming sense of accomplishment when the jury had said, "Not guilty," and to an extent I had, but there was a crucial element missing: joy. The win hadn't changed anything because all I'd wanted to do was celebrate it with my family, hundreds of miles away.

Once I'd left the courthouse, I'd returned to my office, packed my things, and drafted a letter of resignation, which I'd left on Alan's desk. Then I'd called my dad and had asked him to come down to the city to help me move. The next morning, he'd arrived with a box truck, and we'd celebrated my big win with a bottle of champagne as we'd packed.

I blinked back tears at the memory, swiping my wrist across my eyes before they could fall. I couldn't recall the last time I'd been so sure about a decision, despite the uncertainty of it. Maybe Alan was right; maybe I was throwing away my potential. Being a small-town general practice attorney definitely wasn't going to be as exciting, but being the best defense attorney in a big city meant nothing if all I had at the end of the day was a promotion or a cold corner office with no one to share it with. The worst that could happen was I gave it a try and decided a small-town legal practice wasn't for me. I could always find another job, but I'd never get back the precious moments with the people I loved. So, here I was in Evergreen Falls, about to start a new chapter, just in time for the New Year.

The savory scent of black-eyed peas wafted into my apartment from the diner downstairs. It was a traditional dish that my parents served every New Years Eve for good luck. Mom had brought up a big bowl for me earlier, and I'd already devoured half of it. With an empowering inhale, I stood and began unpacking my last box.

The familiar cadence of footsteps on the stairs told me my sister was on her way up before she even knocked, so I left the bedroom and called out, "Come in," as she rapped her knuckles against the door.

Aspen entered with a smile. Her wavy brown hair was pulled up in a ponytail, and her green apron was dusted with flour. She must've just finished her shift at the diner. Holidays were always extra busy at the restaurant, so she'd left the kids with her husband in order to help out.

"How's the unpacking going?" she asked, plopping down on my sleek, leather couch that was more aesthetically pleasing than it was comfortable. I'd already added it to the list of items to be replaced.

The fabric squeaked beneath my jeans as I joined her, tucking my legs underneath me. "I'm about done."

"Good. I know I've said it like a million times since you got here yesterday, but I'm really glad you're home."

"Me too," I admitted. "It feels like I can breathe again."

"Gemma won't stop asking me when you're going to come over for a playdate."

I smiled at the mention of my niece. Knowing I'd be around to watch her and my nephew grow up made this move so much sweeter. "Maybe tomorrow."

Aspen gave me a searching look. "Have you spoken to Roger Boone, yet?"

"Briefly, this morning. We're going to meet next week to go over logistics."

"Your own practice. How exciting." She beamed.

"It's going to be different, but I'm looking forward to helping people in our community."

"So, about that..." Aspen twirled her ponytail. "I was wondering if maybe you might need an assistant. Part-time. After we talked on Christmas, I spoke with Danny and he said if I got a job, we could afford daycare, so..."

I cocked my head as I considered her question. "Are you saying you want to work with me?"

She shrugged. "I know I don't have any law experience,

but I've been helping Mom with the business-side of things at the diner for a while, and I'm pretty quick to—"

"Of course," I interrupted what was probably a rehearsed speech to convince me to say yes, but I didn't need to be convinced. "I would love it if you came to work with me."

"Really?"

"Absolutely," I exclaimed. One of the main reasons I moved home was so that I could be around to help my family, so bringing Aspen on only reaffirmed that I'd made the right choice.

Her face lit up. "Thank you. I can't wait to learn from you."

"I didn't realize you we're interested in law."

"You make it sound kinda cool, and, well, I've always looked up to you." Her cheeks turned rosy-pink.

"Really?" I placed a hand over my heart, utterly touched by her words.

"Yeah. You're my big sister."

"Come here." I pulled her in for a hug.

"Okay, okay, that's enough sappiness." She pulled back. "There's something else we have to discuss."

The shift in her tone had me wary. "Why do I feel like I'm going to want a glass of wine for this conversation?"

"Because you're gonna want one. Me, too."

I crossed to the kitchen and opened the bottle of merlot on my counter, then poured two glasses. "Okay, hit me," I said as I returned to the couch and handed Aspen her glass.

Her expression grew serious. "Jake knows you're back."

My pulse quickened at the mention of his name. "That was fast. I just spoke with Mr. Boone a few hours ago."

"Danny told me Jake saw you and Dad unpacking the box truck yesterday."

That made more sense. I let out a breath. "Well, at least he's still respecting my space."

"True. I know you've been busy, but have you given any thought to what you want to do?"

I shook my head. There hadn't been much opportunity to contemplate my love life over the past six days.

After our conversation in the Village Square on Christmas, I'd clued Aspen in on what was going on. She'd listened intently and had held back on advice, respecting that what I'd needed then was to vent.

My sister swirled her glass. "Can I say something?"

"Go for it."

"I know you're hurting now, and that you've been hurt before where he's concerned, so I understand that you're afraid to trust him, but Jake's a solid guy."

I took a sip of my wine.

She continued, "After you guys broke up and you left, you made it very clear that you never wanted to hear anything about him again, so I never brought it up, but..."

"But what?" I leaned closer.

"After Hailey gave birth to Adalyn, she was out at the pub one night, and I was there on a date with Danny. I'd had a few beers, and I didn't exactly hold my alcohol well when I was nineteen, so I decided that was the moment I was going to defend your honor."

I suppressed a laugh as I pictured my little sister stumbling over to berate Hailey Jennings.

"Anyway, I called her some pretty ugly things, and to her credit, she took it all. When I was done, she confessed that she had kissed Jake that night because she knew you were about to walk in, and she wanted to break you up."

I pursed my lips. That was precisely what Jake had told me, and my sister had no reason to lie to me about this.

Aspen continued, "She said she thought Jake belonged with her and since you were going away to school while she and Jake were staying here in Evergreen Falls, she used that party as her opportunity to move in on your man."

I scoffed. "She'd always been a conniving witch."

Aspen drank some of the wine. "I'm not done. Then, she told me Jake had been so angry with her after, that she realized how badly she'd messed up because she would never get her chance with him."

"Except she had his baby, so..."

"Right, well, she brought that up, too. The night they slept together, Jake was out at the bar, and he'd been really upset about something. Hailey manipulated the situation to her advantage thinking that if she could get Jake to...you know...then maybe she'd finally have her chance with him. But then the next morning, he made it explicitly clear that there would never be anything between them because of what she'd done to you. Turns out, the reason Jake was out drinking the night before was because had Hailey not screwed everything up, it would've been his and your anniversary. Apparently, every year on that day he drowns his sorrows and mourns the loss of the love of his life."

My brows shot up. "What?"

"And, yes, that last part is a direct quote."

Oh my God.

Aspen squeezed my hand. "I know it's a lot to take in. I just thought you should know that Jake didn't lie to you. I don't agree with the way he handled the whole your-enemy-is-my-baby-mama situation, but I really believe he wasn't trying to hurt you."

I nodded mutely as my heart constricted with fragile hope. Needing to move, I got up and crossed to the window. The diner overlooked the Village Square, so I had a prime view of the evergreen tree. The ornaments that had hung there the week before were gone. "Aspen, is the wishing tree tradition still a thing?" I asked.

"Yup. Everyone in town will flock there tonight and tie their wishes onto the branches before the fireworks. Why?"

I crossed one arm over my chest and said, "Because I have a wish to make."

NINE

The Village Square was a magical sight filled with twinkling white lights that draped over the bare trees, casting a warm glow over the festive scene. People milled about, bundled up in colorful winter attire, with pink-tinged cheeks and smiles on their faces. The crisp air carried the comforting aroma of the giant evergreen intermingled with the freshly-baked treats from the food vendors. My boots crunched the salt coating the brick pathway as I wandered through the square in search of my family. After she'd left my apartment earlier, Aspen and I had agreed to meet up for the fireworks, but I'd underestimated how many people would be there that evening. The square was alive with the sounds of laughter, chatter, and holiday music. Children ran around with glee, and their excited voices carried through the air. It made me eager to see my niece and nephew.

A woman called out my name, and I turned, immediately spotting Hailey as she approached, her blond hair bouncing against her long down coat. While I realized that interacting with her at some point would be inevitable now that I lived there, I hadn't anticipated having to deal with that on my second day. I folded my arms across my chest and steeled myself, figuring it best to get this over with.

"I'm glad you're here," she said as she stopped in front of me.

Doubtful. I couldn't recall a single time that she and I'd ever had a civil conversation.

When I didn't respond, she cleared her throat. "I heard you moved back to town."

"Mmm hmm." I nodded.

She clasped her gloved hands together and blew out a breath. "I want to apologize to you for the way I treated you when we were younger." Her words took me by surprise. "I was jealous, and I realize that's a terrible reason to have behaved the way that I did, so I'm sorry."

I studied her face, finding remorse in her eyes. I swallowed. "Thank you."

Her gaze dropped to the ground. "I'm not expecting for us to become friends or anything, but I've really tried to become a better person, and it would be great if we could start fresh."

Grateful for her effort, I nodded slowly. "I appreciate you saying that." The truth of it was, Jake mattered to me, and because of Adalyn, Hailey mattered to him, so if he and I were going to give things an earnest shot, then I would have to figure out a way to move past my disdain for Hailey Jennings.

"Daddy, higher," a little girl squealed, drawing our attention to the tree where Jake had his giggling daughter perched on his shoulders as she stretched to hang her wish on a branch. My heart swelled at the sight.

"Your daughter seems wonderful," I said. My version of an olive branch.

"She's the best." Hailey's harsh features softened as she watched her little girl. "Jake's a really good dad."

I nodded. "I always figured he would be."

Hailey sighed. "He really loves you, Laurel."

I rubbed my lips together, and returned my attention to Jake who was presently engaged in what appeared to be a tickle fight with his six-year-old. I couldn't help but grin.

"Don't hurt him," Hailey muttered as she walked away.

My pulse raced as I strode toward the only man I'd ever loved. Jake's laughter faded as he noticed me emerging from the crowd, and he set Adalyn down.

"Hi," I said, stopping in front of him.

"Hi." His expression was unreadable.

I offered a tentative smile and his eyes brightened.

"I remember you from my Christmas pageant," the little girl announced proudly.

"You have a great memory." I crouched so I was at her level. "Did you hang your wish on the tree?"

She nodded animatedly and pointed toward the top of the tree. "I put it as high as my daddy could reach. I wanted to hang it at the tippy tippy top, but Daddy said the wind is much stronger up there so it might blow away."

I chuckled at Jake's ingenuity. "That's a very good point." Although I had no doubt that Jake would've used a ladder from the fire truck to get up to the very top if that was what his daughter had really wanted.

"Do you have a wish?" she asked.

I stood as I replied, "I do."

"You and Daddy should hang your wishes together. But not too high up 'cause the wind."

I glanced at Jake. "Good idea."

The little girl tugged on the bottom of her dad's coat. "Oh, there's Ruby. Can I go play with her?"

Jake's eyes followed where she was pointing. "Sure, but you have to stay near her Mommy, okay? There's too many people here tonight for you to be wandering off."

She stretched out her pinky. "Promise."

Jake hooked his little finger with hers. "Have fun."

Adalyn rushed toward her friend like she was competing in a race, and I laughed.

Jake shook his head. "I wish I had ten percent of her energy."

"You and me both."

Now that we were alone, the tension grew palpable.

Jake tucked his hands into the back pockets of his jeans. "So, I hear you moved back."

I nodded. "I'm going to take over Roger Boone's law practice."

He cracked a smile. "Wow. That'll be different than what you're used to."

"Maybe that's not such a bad thing."

"Maybe you're right."

Last we spoke, he'd made it clear that the ball was in my court, so this was my moment to be brave. "I'm sorry I doubted you."

His brows drew together.

"I know you were telling the truth about what happened the night of the party, and I'm sorry I doubted you."

He removed his hands from his pockets and used one to stroke his beard.

"If I hadn't..." I trailed off. "Well, there's no use dwelling on things we can't change."

"You're right." Jake nodded slowly as he gazed up at the illuminated wishing tree, filled with countless hopes for the future.

I wrapped my arms around myself. "You're the only man I've ever loved, Jake Hansen."

He fixed his familiar brown eyes on me, and his lips turned up in the corners. "And you're the only woman I've ever loved."

I took a deep breath before continuing. "I have no idea what the future holds, but I really hope that yours and mine are intertwined."

Jake pulled a piece of paper on a string out of his pocket. After reading the wish to himself, he handed it to me. I squinted to read his scribble, which had always been notoriously messy.

I wish for another chance with the love of my life.

I sniffled to hold back the tears that were threatening to fall as my gloved hand fumbled around my pocket to find my wish. When I did, I handed him the paper, and as he read it, I recited the words I'd written. "I wish for a life with my one and only love."

He stared at it for a moment before meeting my eyes. His were glistening, much like mine were. "Shall we?" He gestured toward the tree. I found a solid branch and tied his wish to it, and he tied mine right beside it.

He faced me. "I've missed you so damn much."

Unable to stop myself, I threw my arms around him. Jake pulled me close and buried his face in my hair.

"I'm sorry," I whispered. "For everything."

Jake gently cupped my face in his hands. "Me, too."

I lost myself in his warm brown eyes, seeing the same love and longing that I felt bursting within me. Before I could overthink things or get self-conscious about the whole town watching, I rolled onto my tiptoes and let my lips connect with his. The kiss was sweet and filled with the promise of more—when we didn't have an audience. He pressed his forehead to mine, and I cupped the wiry hair dotting his chin.

"I've never stopped loving you," he murmured, voice husky with emotion.

"I love you, too. I always have," I whispered back.

Like a scene from a movie, the fireworks started, lighting up the night sky, and we both laughed. Jake pulled me in front of him, and draped his arms around me, holding me close as we turned our faces upward, mesmerized by the kaleidoscope of colors. As he held me, making me feel safe in his arms, I reflected on the journey that had gotten us to that moment. Somehow, we'd lost ourselves amidst the chaos of life, yet we had found our way back to each other, and I had faith that we'd be stronger and more resilient than before. They say man plans and God laughs, and while I'd certainly learned that lesson, sometimes we get our wishes, too.

I was perched precariously on a rickety wooden chair that was probably older than I was, broomstick in hand, swatting at the blaring smoke detector on the ceiling of my office. "Oh, come on," I shouted at it as though that would make a difference. It didn't. This wasn't how I'd envisioned ending my Friday. After a few more fruitless whacks, I paused to catch my breath, wiping sweat from my brow with the back of my hand. The chair wobbled beneath me, and I grabbed the bookcase to steady myself. "You stupid thing," I muttered through gritted teeth, taking aim once more, but the smoke detector continued its relentless assault on my eardrums, oblivious to my efforts.

I was so focused on my task that I didn't hear Jake come in. Not until he called up to me, amusement coloring his voice. "Whoa there, sweets. What are you trying to do?"

I startled, nearly toppling from my perch, and grabbed the bookcase once more. I looked over to find Jake standing in the doorway. His brown eyes crinkled at the corners as he grinned up at me, seeming far too delighted by my predicament.

"I think it needs new batteries," flustered, I shouted over the noise.

"Come down before you hurt yourself. I'll take care of it." He ducked out of the office, returning moments later with a step ladder from his truck.

I shook my head ruefully as Jake positioned the ladder beneath the shrieking little disk and climbed up. Something fell out of the pocket of his hoodie, and I bent to pick it up. Upon realizing what it was, I gasped and about dropped it like a hot piece of coal.

Jake's capable hands made short work of removing the device from the ceiling. As soon as it was disconnected, blissful silence descended, but I hardly noticed that thanks to the pounding of my pulse in my temples. "There. All better," Jake declared as he climbed down. Once on the ground, he turned and froze at the sight of me holding the jewelry box. His brown eyes grew big, and his hand came up to stroke his beard. I could see the wheels turning in his head as he tried to come up with something to say, but I beat him to it.

"What's this?"

Jake's cheeks flushed pink. "That was supposed to be a surprise for this weekend," he replied, his voice gentle yet flustered. We were going to spend a couple of nights at the Creek View Inn bed and breakfast in Whippleton where our second chance had begun.

My heart pounded against my ribs. "A surprise?"

He nodded, as he reached for the small velvet box, and I let him take it. "So much for that."

"Jake," I whispered.

He sighed. "I had this whole romantic thing planned but screw it." He dropped to one knee.

My hand flew to cover my mouth and my eyes glazed over with tears.

"Laurel, these past few months with you have been better than I could've dreamed. I'm so proud of what you've accomplished as you've re-invented your life here. Your dedication to the things you're passionate about—like your career and your family and this town—is truly inspiring. You pour that same commitment into our relationship, and I couldn't be more grateful." He cleared the emotion in his throat. "Not only have you blown me away with your love, but you've embraced my daughter as if she were your own." Jake wiped a tear from his cheek. "You've always been an amazing and supportive partner, but seeing you flourish as a mother-figure to Adalyn has made me fall more in love with you than I ever thought possible."

I blinked to clear my vision.

"I love you, Laurel. I've *always* loved you. We may have gotten a little lost along the way, but if you'll let me, I'll spend the rest of my life making up for that." He flipped open the box. "Will you be my wife?"

A sob escaped my throat as I nodded feverishly, my emotions rendering me unable to speak. Jake slid my grand-mother's ring onto my shaking finger, then stood. I managed to whisper his name as I stared, transfixed by the pear-shaped diamond sitting atop a dainty gold band.

"Your Grampy gave it to me a few weeks ago when I asked him and your parents for their blessing."

I tossed my arms around him and squeezed. "I love you so much." We held each other tight, and a profound sense of rightness settled over me.

Jake's lips found mine and we sank into a deep, passionate kiss. All the years of longing and heartache seemed like a far distant memory. Maybe that was because

I'd always belonged to Jake Hansen, and now we were going to make that official. My hands roamed over his muscular back and broad shoulders as our kisses grew more heated. Needing to feel his skin on mine, I snaked my hands up under his hoodie. Mirroring my desire, Jake's calloused fingers deftly undid my blouse and slipped it from my shoulders before flicking open the clasp on my bra.

I'd given up on wearing my shapewear a while ago. It only made getting undressed take longer, and Jake and I spent a lot of time without our clothes on. I didn't know if we'd always be so ravenous, or if we were just making up for the years we'd been apart, but I was more than happy to indulge our hunger.

Jake grasped my breasts and bent his mouth to my nipples, taking the time to savor each one, and I tossed my head back, letting my hair hang as I gripped the edge of my desk for support. His hands slid up under my skirt and he dragged my panties down to my knees. I wiggled my legs so that they dropped to the floor, then I kicked them away. His lips found the crook of my neck as his palms explored my supple body. I no longer tensed when Jake roved over my midsection. Any worries I'd had about my fiancé [insert exciting squeal here] not finding me attractive had long ago been squashed.

His fingertips dug into my hips as he dropped to his knees and stuck his head up my skirt. I grabbed the hem and lifted it so I could watch as his tongue lapped up my seam. "You always taste so good, sweets." He moaned with appreciation as his tongue slid between my folds in search of my aching bud. I didn't know if it was because Jake and I had learned about sex together, but he always knew exactly how to touch me to get me to come. His lips closed around my clit, and he gently sucked while his tongue drew circles around the tip.

My legs shook and I gripped my desk for support as my body quivered on the precipice. Jake hummed, sending a jolt of vibration through me, and I was done for. Dropping my skirt, I clutched my desk with both hands as I writhed on his face, fighting to keep from falling. His fingers kneaded my backside, holding me in place as I rode out my orgasm. I exhaled shakily as Jake got up and pressed a kiss to my lips, transferring some of my juices from his beard to my chin. I reached up to wipe his facial hair, but he jerked away.

"You know I like to smell you on me after."

I rolled my eyes. "You say that every time."

"Because it's true. There's nothing sexier than having your scent linger. It's such a satisfying tease."

My fingers went to the button zipper on his jeans. "If you say so." I reached through the opening and freed his erection. "My turn." I crouched in front of my man and wrapped my lips around his bulbous head.

"Fuck, Laurel," he groaned as he gathered up my hair and wrapped it around his fist.

My tongue traced around his shaft as I took him deep into my mouth, sucking my cheeks in as I went. Jake guided my pace, and I widened my jaw to take more of him. After a few strokes he plucked me off and pulled me to my feet. "I need your pussy." He scooped behind my thighs and lifted me onto my desk, then lined himself up at my entrance. My fingernails danced over his abs as he slid easily into my wet channel until he was fully seated. I traced the hard lines of his muscles, marveling at how perfectly we fit together, while I lifted my legs and crossed my ankles behind him for stability. He held onto my shoulders and worked into a steady rhythm at an angle that hit my g-spot precisely, sending the most pleasurable sensations through my nerves. Judging by the satisfied smirk on his face, he knew it, too. Before long, my muscles clenched, and I grabbed onto his biceps for support. "Jake," I cooed, as he worked me to the brink.

"That's my girl," he whispered. "Give me what's mine." His words were my undoing and I tumbled into my second orgasm.

Jake pounded into me faster, dragging out my pleasure and bringing about his own. "Fuck," he gritted through his teeth as he stilled, filling me with his love. His forehead dropped to mine and we both held still as we caught our breath.

"I love you," I whispered.

"I love you, too, future wife."

That made me blush. "I like that."

"So do I."

With reluctance, I dropped my legs. "We should probably get cleaned up before—"

The bells on the front door jingled and my heart about stopped. I scrambled toward my discarded clothes, while mentally chastising myself for not locking the door.

"Laurel?" Percival's distinctively nasal voice carried from the lobby.

"Be right there," I shouted as I put my blouse on inside out. With amusement, Jake gestured for me to fix it before pulling on his hoodie.

After taking a second to smooth over my hair, I opened my office door and stepped into the entry. "How are you doing today, Percival?" I asked, trying not to come off as scattered as I felt.

"Oh, my. Perhaps you should turn on your air conditioner. You look...warm."

With that, Jake emerged from behind me.

Percival's plump cheeks reddened and his eyes glinted with realization. "Ah, hello, Jake."

"Hi, Percival."

"Jake was just, umm, helping me with my smoke detector. There was a little mishap."

"I see," he replied with his lips turned into a teasing smirk. "Well, don't let me interrupt." He adjusted his bowtie.

"It's fine. What brings you by today?" I asked. Percival had taken to visiting me several times a week ever since I'd taken over for Roger, so the likelihood of this simply being a friendly drop-by was high.

"I've just left Ed Miller's ranch, and I'm afraid he's in a bit of a conundrum."

"What kind of conundrum?" I asked as I leaned against the reception desk and crossed my arms over my chest.

"You're aware that he allows people to board the horses in his barn."

I nodded.

"Apparently, one of the boarders is convinced that Ed's barn is haunted, and now he wants a refund on his boarding fees," Percival divulged as he removed his summer coat and draped it over his arm. "I told Ed that he won't be required to refund the man's money, but the boarder is threatening to sue if he doesn't."

I pressed my lips together to stifle a laugh. When I'd moved back to Evergreen Falls, a part of me thought having a small-town law practice might be boring, but I'd been sorely mistaken. "You're correct. A haunted barn isn't grounds for a refund."

"Yes, I know, but this boarder is apparently causing quite the stink. He's threatening to tell the other boarders, so Ed is worried. He wants to hire one of those ghost psychics like on the television. Do you know any?"

Beside me, Jake coughed to cover up his laughter.

"Tell Ed not to worry. I'm going away for the weekend, but I'll give him a call on Monday, and help him sort this mess out."

"He will indeed be pleased to hear that. Thank you, Laurel."

"Of course."

"Where are you off to?"

"Jake and I are staying at a little bed and breakfast. Actually, we're celebrating—"

"Laurel being back in Evergreen Falls for six months," Jake interjected and I eyed him curiously.

"Ahh, do enjoy yourselves. I'll get out of your hair." He waved goodbye.

Once he was gone, I turned to Jake. "What was that about?"

"If you tell Percival we're engaged, the entire town will know before we've even had a chance to tell our families the good news."

"Good call." I placed a palm on his chest and admired how my ring sparkled in the light. "What would I do without you?"

His strong arms encircled my waist as he replied, "You'll never have to find out." Then, he pressed a kiss to my forehead, sealing his promise, and filling me with the most reassuring sense of contentment because in this crazy little town, with this man by my side, I had everything I'd ever need.

NEXT STEPS

Want a Bonus Epilogue from Jake & Laurel?
Get it now for free by going to www.kayekennedy.com/
laurel

Help others fall in love with Jake & Laurel by leaving a
review on Retailers, BookBub, and GoodReads.

Want more Small-Town Holiday Romance?

PUMPKIN SPICE & PROPHECIES

A Grumpy/Sunshine Small-Town Halloween Romance

Podcaster Shaunie Ross believes in ghosts, ghouls, and
happily ever afters, but her infuriating co-host, Harrison,
believes in none of the above. When their Halloween
special takes them to a small New England town brimming
with haunted lore, Shaunie stumbles into a prophecy from

the local psychic matchmaker that goes viral overnight. Suddenly, she's pressured into a staged romance with the town's pumpkin patch bachelor, while Harrison simmers on the sidelines. But as fake sparks fly and real jealousy burns, Shaunie begins to wonder if the prophecy was never about the farmer at all, but about the one man she swore she'd never fall for.

You can interact with Kaye, chat all things romance, and get access to freebies in her exclusive **Facebook Group**: **Romance Reads that Kiss & Tell**

Join Kaye's Romance Readers Club and be the first to find out about new releases and giveaways! You'll also get free bonus scenes and fun extras.
Sign up at www.kayekennedy.com

ACKNOWLEDGMENTS

Without the following individuals, this story may never have been told:

• My grandmother for fostering my love of reading from a young age and for always being my number one fan—no matter what I do. Also, for always making Christmas special and for keeping traditions alive.

• Krystal for being the best author assistant/cheerleader/friend.

• Jaycee DeLorenzo for bringing my vision for the cover to life.

• My KATs (members of my Facebook Group) for your loyalty, understanding, kind words, and support.

• My author friends for cheering me on with enthusiasm when I decided to publish a holiday story two days before Christmas.

• YOU for taking a chance on love with my characters.

ALSO BY KAYE KENNEDY

<u>Small Town Holidays Series</u>

If you loved *Merry Ex-Mas*, then this is your series! Feel-Good Standalone stories set in small towns during the holiday seasons

Pumpkin Spice & Prophecies – Shaunie & Harrison

<u>Burning for the Bravest Series</u>

If you like alpha males with soft centers who love hard and make love harder, then this series featuring New York City firefighters is for you!

Burning for More – Dylan & Autumn

Burning for This – Jesse & Lana

Burning for Her – Ryan & Zoe

Burning for Fate – Jace & Britt

Burning for You – Kyle & Allie

Burning for You: The Wedding – Kyle & Allie

Burning for Love – Declan & Gwen

Burning for Trouble – Mack & Tori

Burning for Secrets - Brix & Georgia

Burning for Reality - Theo & Kenzie

Burning for Christmas - Keith & Brielle

Standalone set in the same world

<u>Flirting with the Finest Series</u>

Follow the men and women of the Special Investigations Task Force in New York City as they fight crime and fall in love.

Flirting with Forever – Hunter & Lauren

Flirting with Fame - Tai & Bellamy

Flirting with Faith - Erik & Aubrey

Flirting with Freedom - Cooper & Leila

<u>**Rescued by the Rangers Series**</u>

Follow a team of former Army Rangers turned independent contractors who've taken on the most challenging missions, but have struggled to find love. Until now.

Rescuing Griffin - Prequel to Book 1

Rescued by Chance – Griffin & Holly

Rescued by Loyalty — Nick & Mia

ABOUT THE AUTHOR

Kaye Kennedy is the author of contemporary romance and romantic suspense novels featuring everyday heroes who love hard and make love harder. Fun fact: she used to be a firefighter and now she writes about them! If you like steamy and soulful reads that will break your heart and put it back together again, then her stories are for you. In her books, you can always expect a happily ever after that kisses and tells.

She earned her degree in English Literature and taught college composition & literature classes before switching gears entirely and becoming an entrepreneur, starting multiple businesses. In addition to writing, Kaye sees clients as a psychic medium and serves as a coach for authors wanting to level up their careers.

While originally from New York, Kaye has lived in New Hampshire and Florida, but now calls Connecticut home. She is battling an invisible illness and resides with her rescue mutt turned service dog, Zeus, who is a character in *Burning for Secrets*. Kaye's real-life HEA is her favorite trope: friends-to-lovers (and will one day be turned into a book). When she isn't writing, she's out paddling on the water, indulging in a beach read, checking out a brewery, or feeding her wanderlust.

You can interact with Kaye and get access to freebies in her exclusive Facebook Group: Romance Reads that Kiss & Tell. If you really want to be entertained, check her out on TikTok @authorkayekennedy.

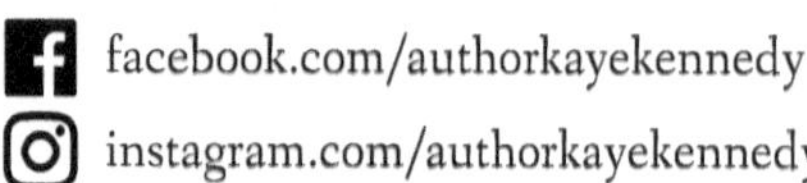

facebook.com/authorkayekennedy

instagram.com/authorkayekennedy